I0763148

A young woman in the Rocky Mountains, separated from the ancestral rhythms of her home in Scotland, turns to ancient rituals to find solace and connection.

Homesickness takes many forms. Occupied by little more than online video captioning she calls "kitten work," our narrator becomes fascinated by the not-long-gone life of her Scottish ancestors, a time when the lamplighter took the night off for the full moon, girls bathed their faces in morning dew, and people sang to the seals.

Her husband, however, is unsure of the emotional efficacy of cooking by candlelight, peeing in the woods, and writing vexed letters to the mayor about the birds living in the doomed aspens behind their apartment building. Especially because the letters are being read, out loud, at the town meetings attended by unimpressed neighbours. But our narrator is bewitched by the liminality of memory.

In a novel of compelling poetic precision and depth, Ross captures the lengths we go to for connection when we're alone, following threads of personal history and fascination to conclusions one can only reach when there's too much time on one's hands and it's too cold to go outside.

Praise for *Hovel*

"Both earthly and otherworldly, full of hard and soft edges, *Hovel* is a book of blunt truths, close looking, and great feeling."

—Amina Cain, author of *A Horse at Night: On Writing*

"This book will stay with me for the longest time. Perhaps I'll pass it on to my descendants. Yes, perhaps this book will help someone in the future understand what true connection is. The protagonist's efforts to overcome the feeling of homesickness and dislocation through small chores and more than anything else: through her senses, observations and willingness to connect to all things living, are so strong. There's a stamina, a subtleness, a poetic beauty and a great sense of timing at play here. On top of that Ailsa Ross shows a strong observational talent, and a lovely sense of humour. And sadness. All in all, I just loved *Hovel*. I just loved everything about it, and on top of that I promised myself that one day—soon—I'll rent that cottage in Northern Scotland. I will just sit there in my 'hovel' and reconnect. It was a wonderful read, Ailsa Ross. Thank you."

—Dorthe Nors, author of *A Line in the World*

hovel

hovel

A Novel

Ailsa Ross

First edition published 2026

The authorized representative in the EU for product safety and compliance is Penguin Random House Ireland, Morrison Chambers, 32 Nassau Street, Dublin D02 YH68, Ireland, https://eu-contact.penguin.ie

Library and Archives Canada Cataloguing in Publication
Title: Hovel : a novel / Ailsa Ross.
Names: Ross, Ailsa, author.
Identifiers: Canadiana (print) 20250220555 | Canadiana (ebook) 20250221403 | ISBN 9780771013485 (hardcover) | ISBN 9780771013539 (EPUB)
Subjects: LCGFT: Novels.
Classification: LCC PS8635.O65853 H68 2026 | DDC C813/.6—dc23

Cover design by Kelly Hill
Cover art: (sheep) Alfred Morris, (type) Maurice Lorrain / Artvee
Typeset in Goudy Oldstyle Std by Erin Cooper
Printed in Canada

Published by Strange Light
An imprint of Penguin Random House Canada
320 Front Street West, Suite 1400
Toronto, Ontario, M5V 3B6, Canada

penguinrandomhouse.ca

10 9 8 7 6 5 4 3 2 1

‘We lived in close proximity to shit.
It made us laugh.’
—Annie Ernaux, *The Years*,
translated by Alison L. Strayer

Contents

WINTER

Late Summer

There are many ways to spend your time. You can watch a crow until you see the red insides of her mouth. If she's flying away, find another crow. If there are no crows, take a mirror and look at the red insides of your mouth. Or if there are no mirrors, close your eyes and think of the Arctic reindeer, their eyes that turn from gold in summer to blue in winter.

Of course, you may hate winter, and that is your right. Then go thinking about the Roman town of Beneventum where, around seventeen hundred years ago, a consul named Tanonius Marcellinus did something so exhilarating for the people they inscribed a stone officially thanking him for the good deeds by which he went rescuing the population from endless boredom.

What toy or entertainment or herd of animals did he introduce?

It may have been that, upon his suggestion, the children went paddling each morning in the Sabato river that still slings pale green past the houses. But there is no record of Marcellinus having been an unofficial swim coach.

Perhaps he was leading the women into shady woods filled with boars. He was bending down the pine boughs and guiding their tongues along sharp needles so they could rate each one on a scale of *tastes like oranges* to *tastes like turpentine*.

Or all the town, all at once, was putting down their scythes and following him up to the top of Vitulano Hill. Marcellinus looked up at the sun, then down at the people. He uttered three words, and then they were bending their legs and looking through the peephole between their calves. Now everything, the upside-down woods and the river and hills, was new. The world was so new.

Yet this version of events does not ring quite true. How many people in those days had the time to put down their tools and walk many miles for pleasure? I must find out how Marcellinus did it. Then I can help myself out of this drifting feeling.

Making the world new should not be so difficult given where I am. I'm far from home, so there is much that is still unfamiliar to me.

I'm no longer in the north of Scotland where pear trees blossom in February and cabbages go shining in gardens all year. Where I live now is very different. There are no crops and the two seasons are rough and pounding.

So I live in a small apartment on a gloomy corner of this long, shadowy town that curves so resolutely around the train tracks. So I have not much of a job and only one friend, and there are no fields and baby chickens are banned.

While the seals and soft sheep are far away now, they are still there. And I am quite healthy; there are wolves padding along the river braids and I am quite well. I am quite well and if I go squinting, this town when viewed from the hill above looks like a crescent moon. It looks like a crescent moon and at night the stars are blooming, they're blooming and I can learn to roam like a contented animal. If I stop being so emotional, I might place my heart here.

Slammakin

September 1

They say that up here in the mountains, human sadness occurs partly because there's not enough serotonin in our heads. There's less oxygen in the mountain air and that affects our brain chemistry. That affects our moods and then we're really not happy.

At this altitude, there's a higher risk of suicide that's tied to the elevation. To find this out, scientists tested the impact of thin air on rats. At four-thousand five-hundred feet, the females grew quite depressed.

Here the air is thin and my nose bleeds often as a result. There's also mould in this unloved apartment building. Sara upstairs has been emailing the local politician about her coughing children, but he's not done a thing about it. So far he's only sent her a detailed explanation about the workings of the free market. I think she's still biting her arm hairs.

It can be sad here with all the coughing children, with the cost of everything and the transient nature of the population—all those new faces are up and leaving with the end of each ski season. And there are few places to rent, and what exists is so expensive. The landlords are hiking the rents all the time; there are hardly any laws against it. The cost of living in our place will be thirty per cent more from November. We just got the letter.

To spruce the flat up, of late I've been taking various fallen twigs home from the woods. Their ends are nearly always pronged like birds' feet—you can help them scrape the earth by bending them this way and that. I like seeing them on the windowsill, tugging out black bits from the cracks. They can clean it all up. They can break everything to pieces. The window frames, the door bottoms; I hope they'll claw it all.

Before I started bringing in twigs, I planned to do the place up in sheep fleece. I thought lying on a floor of sheepskin would give me a pleasant sensation. I'd feel like a tick embracing the warm curves of a lamb.

It was a fine idea. And fleeces are free if you know a farmer well—wool currently being of so little value that farm workers are burning piles of them to the ground. They are mixing them with manure and spreading them across the fields instead of preparing them for sale. But if you are an individual buyer without much in the way of rural contacts, they are very expensive. I have no contacts here, so for me they are very expensive. In the end, I only bought a cover for my hot water bottle. Even it ended up being eighty dollars once you added in shipping costs from Vancouver Island. That put me right off my plan. And even if I could afford having fleece rugs and tapestries, it would not change the fact of the mould; it would not stop me lamenting the lack of light as the sun passed by.

It's sad, thinking about all the things I have purchased in an attempt to cheer this place up. The pufferfish-shaped soap dish looked so beautiful when I saw it for sale by the sea. I hate how it looks at me from the bathroom sink. It belongs on a wooden counter beneath a tree.

It's strange; only three generations ago the cheap surfaces I live among were desirable. Great-Granny was so pleased to live amid the new inventions of Formica and linoleum. She'd grown up amid rotting wood and peat hearths. Now I want what she had. I want wood. I want a hearth.

I suppose I would love Formica and linoleum too if I'd grown up in a Sutherland croft with newspaper stuffing every crevice and rain blowing through the roof. The people then were wet and scared. Then the new materials came. They were practically infallible. They were wipe-clean, wonderful. And the names of some of the first designs!

Spindrift
Softglow
Skylark
Mayflower

I don't know so much about Great-Granny. But I know she loved wildflowers. And seals. She went down to the shore as often as she could. She sang there. A low sound hummed from deep inside her. It spooled across the waves. Drifting seals would be listening, then together their songs went coasting.

Does that sound like whimsy?
Seals are curious and respond to music.
They do sing back.

I've never sung to seals. I wasn't on the beach as a youth. In my teens, life centred round the town bridge with the three arches. That bridge was rounded as a pig's back. It was a couple of centuries old by the time we drank under it.

There were herons swishing about on long legs there. Sometimes they stood very still. Then they'd be striking fish in white flashes.

I've read herons have been about for up to sixty million years.
They were by this river before it had a name, before people.

The first people came
Herons watched as they chanted and threw metal objects upon the earth
Blue smoke rose above the first houses
Houses turned into hamlets—
Into a market town

Travellers swept luminous pearls from the banks
One was taken for the royal crown
Then the forces came and banned the practice

The pig's-back bridge came,
And boys and girls and carts and cows began to cross the waters easily

The Great Change came, and to that sleepy vale arrived the beginnings of industry
A stockings factory
A boots factory

Those just as soon came tumbling down
Like the pearl people
Like the old songs

Oil rigs were placed in the nearby sea
And men began to drive cars to work in the nearby city
The lichens on the bridge grew long,
Grew fronds

Herons watched
As young girls, told they were weak in PE
And lazy
Came here at night

The youngest beneath the arches were eleven or twelve

The herons stared as we drank vodka and threw trolleys in the shallow river
Handle-side down
We'd dance on them
We'd stretch our arms towards one another like starfish, like lily petals
Then sway into the toilets by the car park.

The men who'd stood watching by their cars followed us in. We were so excited. Darren had green eyes. It was rumoured he'd been to prison.

Afterwards, we walked to Jade's. Her mum never minded how many teenagers were in the house. Her mum was never there.

We'd make each other tea and loll on the sofa drunkenly plaiting each other's hair. The tv show we watched featured four women in the Big Apple. They swished quilted pouches about the city on chains.

We imagined being those adults—swanky cherries in our mouths, winged shoes on our feet. We'd be so sophisticated, heading into elevators with firefighters and carpenters on our own terms.
We'd be so free.

At home on Sunday mornings, we were acting funny. Now men were following us into the toilets on Saturday nights, we required everything in our power to be absolutely orderly, absolutely clean. Before, we'd been nodding off amid slumpen socks and Forever Friends teddies in our messy bedrooms. We couldn't do that now. As soon as we were home, we were lobbing halter tops and knickers into laundry baskets. We were putting on clean pyjamas and going at every bedroom surface with Mr. Sheen.

With scrunched-up newspapers and pastel dusters, we were putting everything to rights—the CD player, the curling tongs, the Groovy Chick notebooks, the Dior tester perfumes, the Dream Matte Mousse, the Jacqueline Wilson books, the birthday cards, the holiday wedges—we were lifting them all up, wiping them, and setting them back down again. For everything now had to be quite orderly. Everything had to be orderly and then we could not be a schlutt or a schlamp or a slammakin.

Once we were done with our bedrooms, we set about changing ourselves with St. Tropez and tanning mittens. We got rid of everything we didn't want. Our peely-wally skin and thick dark hair; every strand and nail and pit we transformed.

In school we were often getting in trouble with this teacher or that for running blue mascara wands absent-mindedly through our arm hairs while they drew on the blackboards. What mattered, it was clear, was staying as neat as a pin. They weren't likely to give you any trouble for using St. Tropez though. It wasn't any of their business what we did at home. So we all tanned ourselves into oblivion and thought we looked very grown-up for it. The town men liked it. They'd be rolling down their car windows and requesting that we get our rats out as we walked from the chip shop to the river at night.

I think I'm reminded very much of Jade's house in this flat with its stains and its low ceiling. I lose my husband and the puppy as soon as they fall asleep beside me. In the dark I lose them. I'm awake for hours and I can feel the low ceiling coming down till it's Saturday night and we've done up the buttons on our jammy tops all wrong, we've got butter all over the mugs; we can barely see Carrie having sex on screen as we lay our heads on each other's knees.

And now Jade and some other girls are asleep in her room, and me and some others are in the spare room. Her big brother's friends are coming in drunk. I'm pretending to sleep but their tobaccoed hands are pressing in anyway. Clammy fingers and they won't stop.

Under this low ceiling I'm never not in Jade's house. No, I don't think I'll ever not hate this place—no number of fleeces in the world could stop this flat from dredging up things that happened when I was too young to understand them.

I was fortunate compared to the ones living in town. Mum and Dad made a peaceful home in the country for us. I could wander home through stony fields on Sunday mornings. I'd walk along farm tracks, beneath beech trees, and then there'd be the bathroom the kitchen the brass tongs the oil lamps the bannisters the Sheila Maid the wedding pictures the shearing scissors the butter paddles the woodworm doors the door handles clanking softly closed in every room—and every room quiet and every room safe.

Cleaning, cleaning. I hardly do any of that now. I don't like getting too close to the walls. Suppose I am a bit of a schlutt then. Suppose I am quite the slammakin. That's new. The women before me knew how to clean. Great-Granny definitely knew how to clean. She was a chambermaid at The Stromness Hotel. It was a fairly large hotel—grand for an Orkney town. Mhairi Mackay was sixteen when she arrived from Sutherland. Living there all alone, it was her first time away from home. All day she'd be smoothing beds and replacing towels, she'd be polishing taps and wiping mirrors and sweeping out fires and pressing feathers into corners and telling the visiting minister to get his hands off her.

I'm glad she had the seals. I'm glad they listened and sang back. As she bent and swept at ashen grates, it must have been comforting to think about heading down to the beach later to meet them. After work, she was walking past the stone houses and along the sea wall, she was walking to the beach then facing the islands across the water. Beyond the islands, there on the mainland were her siblings, her mother, her father.

And the seals were there. They were always there. They never failed her.

When my husband came home from work this evening, he found me in bed with the soap dish. He came in under the covers. He listened and watched as I furrowed between its pocked ridges with my fingernails. I said I hated it here.

He said when he was sad he went running.
I said, 'I want to run.'
He said, 'Then you should run.'
'No I want to *run*. Why didn't Mum and Dad send me away or something?'

'Being a parent is tough,' he said, playing with the ring on my finger. 'You've got to manage these little developing lives while you too are imperfect. You were a free being, your parents were free beings. Freedom blossoms into all sorts of beautiful and ugly things, especially when the conditions of freedom are all new and unpredictable.' He gently released the soap dish from my hands and said, 'There was nothing like The Bridge when your mother and father were teenagers. In many ways, theirs was a more innocent time. They cannot have known what was happening down there.'

'Don't be reasonable when I'm in a mood and hating everyone. I hate Jim next door, why's he still preying on young Asian girls? Why's Wayne been knocking drunk on our window? I hate these walls. I don't want to be sharing anything with them.'

'I can't help you when you're like this—'

I said he didn't need to. I'd already come up with a plan for helping myself. I'd do various projects until I stopped wanting to leave.

He asked what I'd been doing this week.

I pointed at the soap dish and said, 'I've been cleaning this.'

Softs

September 9

If I was living in a fine house near the creek, I could grow a hedge, tall and green. In the morning I'd drift through the patio doors. I'd tumble beneath the glossy foliage of the hedge's undercarriage then lie in the shadows with the insects. There'd be sun stripes crossing the lawn and broadening. There'd be light falling on our legs, our legs swiping the dewy ground and we'd be rising and they'd be chasing each other through the sky while I rubbed a damp calf with my foot and watched them.

If public spaces felt open to dreaming, I don't think I'd be dreaming of hedges. But what can be done about it? The solution can't be a hedge. There are too few for everybody to have one. And how could I be affording one? Get a different job, then work all hours? I'd have no time for dreaming then.

I exist in a world of 'no loitering' signs. I live amid signs that set up hierarchical stations where the dreamer lies far below the watcher. I live in this time, so to be well I must learn to loiter amid my neighbours. I'll do that. I'll go without shoes to catch more attention. It's a harmless thing, going without shoes. I don't really know why it's viewed with disdain. Only a few generations ago, harmless actions like this were not so suppressed. Singing while walking, doffing one's cap to the sun—that was quite normal where I'm from. So many harmless acts that were once the norm; perhaps I can bring some back.

Though will I really stay so resolute while being watched? Probing eyes have always split me and the ants into separate entities. If there's one neighbour looking, I'll fling every insect into the sun while I hurry to dust myself off and get going again.

I'm not the only one to feel this kind of shame. Malcolm and the rest of the old men could easily be in the grass. They've all the time in the world. But they are only ever in the town café. I think Malcolm should be here. He's not shy. He came over when he heard me talking with Inga at the grocery store. I suppose he must have noticed I had an accent, for a week later he sat down at my table in the café and introduced himself. He handed me a triangle-shaped scone on a plate. Then he was weaving his hands together while speaking misty-eyed of the Battle of Culloden, of the tragic heroism on display during the Jacobite Rebellion. He began humming 'The Skye Boat Song' while swaying with eyes half-closed—it turned out to be the theme tune to his favourite show.

Look Malcolm, I wanted to say while dotting my plate crumbs, I hate Culloden and every other dank moor battle. The myth of state and nation is nothing but a continued fantasy maintained by the collective uniting of our imaginations, and while you may see Bonnie Prince Charlie as some kind of Che Guevara character—as a courageous and most worthy freedom fighter—to others he was nought but a haughty Italian popinjay whose reckless bid for the 'divine' right to rule caused endless suffering to ordinary families. Also, that song you were so evocatively humming? It was not written by a patriotic Scot, *Malcolm*, but a nineteenth-century Englishman.

Malcolm, oh Malcolm, I am not being cruel. I mock you somewhat, but only because my head too is filled with romantic notions about the past. Really I am much moved by how beautifully you can hold a tune. Your voice is quite lovely, and if I was less shy I would press in your hands my copy of the *Carmina Gadelica*. I'd press that haunting chant book of the old incantations against your bony chest; I'd look you in the eye and ask if you wouldn't sing me one of those songs.

I wouldn't mind hearing the old songs, Malcolm. Hum me the one about the brown swans. Do it outside. Sing me the ones for milking cows. Do it where we can slide our fingers up the stalks till they're running.

My husband doesn't think I should assume everyone with time on their hands wants to spend it lying by the creek. But I think Malcolm does want to be here, for he has a body. And bodies grip and experience the world. 'The flesh is at the heart of the world,' Maurice Merleau-Ponty wrote. The flesh is at the heart of the world and the world is at the heart of the flesh and I think the old men would like to be here but they know they can't be. The old men can't just sit quietly beneath the trees. They can't go rubbing their toes on the furry pebbles at the bottom of the stream. And they certainly can't be here alone after three.

I hope one day there'll be lone males squatting peacefully in the water—their big bottoms soaking wet while they splay their hands upon the water's surface and watch minnows darting from their own cool shadows. But the abandoned socks on the shore belong to tiny feet alone, and so the old men can't come here. They can't because the desire for bodily touch has now been firmly placed in the sphere of the sexual. You see it in the letters chosen for the problem pages. They're never about how to catch a bird using a rod fashioned from rowan berries. They're about sex. The desire for touch is related to sex in the public imagination, and so wanting to touch the grass with the hands and feet is seen as something of a perversion. And mothers and fathers don't want the old men touching the grass where their children play. That is how it is. And the old men know that, so they stay at home touching their carpets.

I hate what we've done to the men. And I hate what we've done to those two Croatian zoo bears who are constantly separating each other's hind legs then pushing their mouths deep into each other's pelvic regions. They'd be busy flipping rocks and meadow grazing if they weren't in a zoo, but they are in a zoo so what is there for them to do but go pleasuring each other all day?

The problem pages are always suggesting I should be more like a zoo bear. They're always suggesting I should be touching his crotch four times a week in order to maintain a healthy relationship. My relationship with him matters, but it is not the only one. There is also the relationship between my flesh and the world.

There is everyone's relationship with the world. And I would like to see the old men flattening the grass with their feet. Chatting quietly among the mint, or huddling together in pairs, then unfolding newspapers in the spaces between their knees till perhaps their heads touch as they draw moustaches on horses and a blankness within their hearts opens up into the colour green.

The problem pages should be telling me to watch the wild bears. We practically are bears, once you get beneath the skin. Jordan said so last month, during his medicine walk. He shook his foot and said if you ever get lost in the woods, watch and see what the bears are eating. We can eat everything bears can, he said, for our digestive systems are practically the same. Our whole bodies are practically the same, once you get beyond the skin and fur and claws. Yes, when skinned, beheaded, depawed and left on the rocks by unscrupulous hunters, black bears have been erroneously listed as Jane or John Doe in short-lived murder investigations.

Things used to be different. Dorothy Wordsworth and William watched with delight as Sunday women in the countryside hung their shoes and stockings in bundles on their arms and headed shoeless through the meadows. And weren't those siblings often slipping into barefoot trances themselves? Wasn't each cloud becoming an eye for them? It was sweet. With the shadows of swallows flinging themselves against the sun-bright walls for them. With the ravens calling out and the dome of the sky echoing their calls like musical bells. Being barefoot in the grass, it was a feeling akin to sheaths of silk meeting skin.

What kind of shoes did they have dangling from their arms? Fish skin ones hopefully. Catfish shoes with string for bows.

I imagine all parts of the body have an urge to press into solid things, soft things. Why else would some press powdered fingers upon cool rocks and climb towards the sky? Or press a warm pigeon feather against the cheek, or hold a piece of grey gum under the tongue long after the flavour has gone? When did we have to start wearing hobnail boots? I suppose it began with the factories.

Some big boss in Manchester or Liverpool or Glasgow or Norwich may have spotted the opportunity. Some boss with a red, steaming face and his buttons nearly popping off was looking down on the blackened street from his office window. He was watching the factory workers stumbling through their own piss jizzle as they rushed to work. Sod was watching. Sod was smoothing the wet tips of his moustache and moving over to the interior view of the shop floor; he was looking at the rusting bells and rising steam and all those workers flapping about in broken shoes; he was bringing out endless rolls of onion paper from the cabinet; he was taking a sharpened pencil from its holder and drawing pedals and rollers. He was sketching a machine that could fasten uppers to soles with metal pins. He was picking his ear and drawing a machine for cutting leather. He was spitting out tobacco curls then sketching a contraption for rolling materials ever thinner and wider. They could all work. With the power of coal and steam, they could all really work.

Of course, his machine-made shoes would not fit as well as the cobbler's shoe. They'd pinch and squeeze all twenty-six bones of the delicate human foot—they'd add bunions and blisters. But if he got the price right, all those workers down there could buy new pairs. They'd buy from him. All the workers would, all over the country.

Sod was running numbers down the sides of the paper. If he kept wages down low—yes, if he kept the margins very wide by paying each worker far less than the value of each product—oh he'd be rich. My giddy, the riches. He might even convince the country people they needed special shoes for Sundays. With the right campaign, yes he'd convince them their children needed shoes for playing in the summer grasses! It would take a while to change their ways of course. For tradition was so dear to them. But once you were in their heads and you had them feeling ashamed of the old ways, you'd caught them and their families forever. Oh if he got things right, there was spectacular wealth coming to his family. His great-great-grandchildren might be singing from the saloons of Kensington till their death day.

Well I hate Sod, I hate shoes and I hate carpets and I hate the 'no shirts no shoes no service' sign posted in the door of the town grocery store. That sign makes me feel so bad now I'm outside looking at it. Yet no one is going to look. No one is going to point to the poster when my trousers are swishing around my calves like big bells. With this material trailing around my toes, anyone who happens to take a look will simply assume I'm wearing boots.

Walking among the aisles of pink wafers and bulging cartons, nobody is looking; hands are busy curling round boxes of cereal and juice and no one is batting an eye.

When Inga was a child in the Maritimes, she liked to go to the dairy aisle of the grocery store in summer. There she'd slip off her jelly shoes and touch the tiles. The cool, hard feeling of them, she said it was sensational.

It is sensational.

Here I am in the dairy aisle and the feeling is sensational.

That shopper at the end of the aisle is holding his trolley conspicuously near his body. What is he hiding amid those steely shadows?

He's privately pressing his warm feet against cool tiles?
Toe then ball then heel,
Toe ball heel?

After all, these tiles do feel good, as cool as cucumbers.
These tiles are as cool as cucumbers.
And this is a top-ten feeling.
My face in the aisle mirror as I glance past the milk cartons, it's not frowning.

Dook

September 15

My husband is away at his mother's, but I didn't want to drive twelve hours there and back to visit with him. Instead I'm spending the weekend here with Inga. This is our favourite spot to camp in. It's just outside the park.

I feel this spot is Russian-looking, though I've never been to Russia. It's just that I first read *Family Happiness* on this lakeshore. Now I cannot separate Tolstoy's birches and mountains from the birches and mountains here.

Actually the area looks very different now the heat has reached it. Now the meadow we put up our tents in is brown and the paths have grown rutted and dry, it's not like the Siberia of my imagination. Flies are hovering across the lakeshore, our dogs are blowing about the skinny trees and it's hot. It's so hot that if I ignore the glaciers on the mountains above our heads, I can pretend we're in a desert. While Inga lies sunbathing on her damp towel, I've been looking resolutely at my feet and the silver clay between my toes. When I swing my head up to the endless white sky, that's it, I'm in Arizona.

I've never been to Arizona and I've never been to Siberia but it's nice amid the mica. Women in hot places dip their scarfs in it. There are girls who paint their lips with it. When I lie down, I can rim my ear-shells silver with it. Mica diamonds in the tips of my hair; I've been flicking them off with sparkling fingers and trying hard not to cry.

What's making me tug at my hem like a fishing line? What's making me want to press myself against Dad's photos with flattened palms till I'm beside him?

I thought I'd swim and swim here. I thought I'd swim until I was a body in the world. Instead I'm sitting here crunching blood jewels left by the horse flies on my arms. I'm pretending I'm in a desert when I could be beside him.

They're going to leave those lumps shining fervently behind his ear. I'm scared those lumps will grow more.

Suppose I could sit in the shallows. I could lay my head against the warm buttons of the puppy's spine while she thrums like a motorboat.

When I got in the water just now the puppy ran into the woods.

I sat in the shallows and held on to my knees.

Inga came over and said I looked like a baby in the bath. She said I'd be happier if I just swam. I said it was so cold.

We went in together.

Floating on my back, my skin was switching on. Tipping my head back, I could feel my hair, my neck.

Sound waves were sliding by all the watery parts of my body and resounding against the heavy piece of bone just behind my ears. My body was mostly water and my ears were mostly water, and each watery sound wave needed a solid body part to resound against. Now the big bone at the back of my skull was tinkling with fish talking with their teeth. With the chimes of quivering minnows. My skull, soused in softest sounds, was guiding me into other memories of echoes. I was floating into a church shaped like a violin. Into a gallery. Into the back of the car.

My legs jangling from side to side as Mum and Dad and I stream past fields into town. As we get out amid gulls on the rooftop of the shopping centre. Gulls following us along grey streets as our hands fill with bags from BHS, from Benetton and C&A, as we go up past the bakery past the kilt shop past Boots.

With me in the middle,
My parents are raising me with their arms,
Up to the gulls in a game of
One, Two, Three
Weeeeeeee.

Then we're heading breathlessly into the gallery café for cappuccinos and Orangina.

I'm swinging my legs and playing with the fruity bottle. Through it I see palm trees swaying.

Then we're swinging once again
Into the atrium.

We're moving across diamond tiles
I touch black ones only
For everything is a game
As we head up the marble staircase
We're rising from the bottom of a canyon
Sounds of shoes and voices soaring
Up up
Around granite pillars
Past white leaf railings
Sounds fast as tiny birds
Hit the glass sky dome
And disperse as feathers

They're floating down softly now.

We're listening, and feel we're floating on water.

We're standing in front of a girl walking into a gold frame with a line of geese.

We're looking at a woman who was painted many years ago.

I like her ruched red dress. I like her lovely big nose.

And here is a gleaner with her bundle of straw held high on her shoulder.

I like her centre parting all neat beneath her kerchief. I like her dark feet.

Mum is taking my small hand in hers. She's saying, 'This painter lived in France a long time ago.' She leans forward and points to the numbers at the bottom of the gilt frame. 'See? That says 1875.'

'Do you know what a gleaner is?' she is asking.

I'm shaking my head.

'In this picture, the girl is not harvesting her own grain—she is *gleaning* what she can from the farmer's field. He has already taken what he can sell. What's left belongs by law to the people. Their winter will not be easy. See the blue shadows creeping across the fields? It will be cold soon, and what will grow then? Yet do you see how the girl's chin is jutting out, how she appears to be looking directly at you? Her fists are clutching the grain on her shoulder. She's not about to give up. And nor is she ashamed of her status, for she knows she has nothing to be ashamed of.'

She points to the farmer's haystacks behind the girl. 'When the wealthy people in France first saw this series of paintings, they did not like them. How proud Breton had made the peasants look! When they looked at this girl, it made the rich afraid. It made them realise they did not have as much power as they liked to imagine, for though they outranked the poor in terms of wealth, they were far outnumbered. And if the people rose up? It was clear what could happen,' she says.

'What could happen?'

Inga and I spent the rest of the day going in and out of the water. When night came, we swam into sequins of moonlight. We held on to a floating trunk of red cedar with our arms. This drifting log Inga was now standing on, I was almost on; it was rolling beneath our feet like a can opener. Stars were landing like birds on the ocean. I asked if she had memories of being a child while in water. 'I remember hopping from baby berg to baby berg across the sea in springtime,' she said, running along the wet log. I could see her red hair then.

Early Autumn

Berries

September 18

Given the current season, I like to think of all the foragers being busy bees across the northern hemisphere. Gatherers in green socks and shiny shoes are collapsing in moss and stuffing all kinds beneath their hats. Yes across the north, the fruits of the plants and trees are creating a beautiful unity to human action—and though the air is blowing at different temperatures and densities across the continents, it's the season of berry picking from here to Hokkaido, and boots are touching mud and hands are touching berries while there's still time.

Hats are dropping from heads and onto paths with quick nods. They're kicked about. Now a cherished cloche sits upturned on the ground where it acts as a makeshift basket. One hand goes feeling through abundant leaves towards prickliest stems. There's wincing. Some cursing. Then a fist rises triumphantly filled with glassy berries.

A boater fills up. Just enough, and the rest are left for the birds.

Once she's picked her fill, the gatherer gets down on her knees. She carefully bends the crown of her head into the bowl of her beret. Her hands tug felted wool down towards her ears. She stands unsteadily at first, for secrets are now bouncing above her skull. Then she wipes her hands briskly on her skirt, strides through sun-splashed woods, and lets her eyes cast for anything blue or crimson.

Inga and I have been champing at the bit to get out all week. As soon as she's done work at 5:15 pm, we've been heading up the tracks with pepper spray.

We've been coming down dusty and mostly empty-handed. We haven't needed to wear our hats. Still, today, nearer the shadier streams we've been finding a few huckleberries.

What we're doing is perfectly legal in many places—for example, it's legal in Sweden and in Finland. There it's perfectly fine to go about with a tongue that looks covered in squid ink all berry season. It's allowed in the old forests that tremble along the edge of Vienna. Gathering, like gleaning, is enshrined in many ancient laws—and I imagine a fair few peasants had to fight for that to happen.

Here in the mountains though, it's forbidden.
Inga likes that it's forbidden.
She says who cares what anyone thinks about us eating two berries a day?
The government did not make the earth, or the rain or sun. It does not represent the people whose cultures are tied to this land. So why should the park superintendent decide if we eat one or two?
Is he God?
No.
He is just a man who works for a fallible system. So what makes him the authority on such vital trifles? If we should be asking anyone for legal permission about eating the fruits, it should be the Anishinaabe, Aseniwuche Winewak, Dane-zaa, Nêhiyawak, Secwépemc, Stoney Nakoda, and Métis who were here long before the superintendents.

As a child, Inga spent all summer picking berries. All summer, I did too. I was walking up and down Fisher Walk in August and placing raspberries in old ice cream tubs. I was sharing berries with my brothers in the garden. When the brambles were bursting I was picking them, then Mum was helping me add them to cake batter. Before that, she was driving me to the strawberry farms. As primary school kids we received seven pounds per crate. We ate most of what we picked, but still went home flashing small notes. We spent the money on magazines and sweets. All these memories come back when I pick fruit.

In a place where even a child is legally barred from picking a berry, what potential memories that could have flourished vanish?

I know the ban on foraging is not the worst law this government has made; still, Inga is refusing to drive for two hours so we can pick three identical berries on Crown land. And I am refusing to buy a punnet of them from the shop.

It is just so much nicer to eat these berries. These fruits that received the same sunlight and water that we did, that we have so much in common with. It's nice to know them.

Inga really doesn't want me to worry about the law. She says it was obviously enacted so egregious violations—such as commercial picking—could be prosecuted, while, in general, people are free to violate the ban in the pursuit of modest enjoyment.

It's not the wardens I worry about though. There are people in this town who'd love to see thimbleberries caught between our teeth. They'd have our guts for garters if they found us in the ditch pulling thorns from our fingers.

You can feel it, can't you, when people despise or hate or pity you.

'Their glassy eyes that don't admit anything so definite as hate. Only just that underground hope that you'll be burnt alive, tortured, where they can have a peep. And slowly, slowly you feel the hate back starting.'

Maybe Jean Rhys was paranoid, writing that. Maybe I'm paranoid. Inga does not say I'm paranoid, like my husband does. She just says I should let people have their frisson of excitement. Anyway, knowing what to pick is serious business. While for now these forest fruits are only supplementary to our diets, there's no guarantee this will always be so. When the Soviet Union fell, Siberians, suddenly without an income, fled to the forest in search of mushrooms. Of course, they had to know which mushrooms to collect and which were poisonous, Inga says. So we must learn about the foods around us too. 'Anyway. How does picking feel?'

When my hands are flowing through these low, sweet bushes, I feel I'm gently combing a child's hair. I feel my ancestors are living again through me.

That's what the ancient Greeks said. We should live as though our ancestors are again living through us.

Now I've touched these berries, and in the moment of plucking I must be three hundred thousand years old. I'm in my thirties normally. I'm not so wise. Even a ninety-year-old who is sitting at her table is young and a little unwise. But if the act of gathering wakes up every ancestor who gathered before us, then in such moments we contain the experiences of everyone—of all the past generations who reached for the earth's fruits.

Also it's mesmerising, the rhythm of it.

Eyeing
Grasping
Twisting
Devouring

I really think that through the body, living takes place. And through the imagination. Through the imagination, on touching these berries, I'm walking amid the clamour of animals and kin; I'm heading up with the children and horses.

Up to those summer huts, simple as shells.

All summer there's us high in the hills. We're in our summer-town, looking down on the winter-town. There the men work, still. And the cows and sheep are growing plump on fresh grasses, and the butter and cheese and children are turning golden-sweet, and wild strawberry patches are quilting the high places. Gifts of fruit and flowers, these life's delights need no tending.

It's not just me dreaming. I come from a long line of dreamers. I see it in my niece; the lights in her eyes flash as she encounters a pond, a cloud, a puddle. It's in my father. His captions are always about *veilings on veilings of mist enfolding the land as dawn breaks softly into the softest of skies*. Great-Uncle grew up in Orkney on the edge of the old times. He too wished for beauty and the past; his poems were about imagined crofter lasses trudging through lavish dung, dreaming of corn stalks and milk—

'And lovers
Unblessed by steeples lay under
The buttered bannock of the moon.'

Give him or Granny a few words—pony and tea, hill and blanket—and their minds were soon spooling stories around voices and hooves.

And George's mentor Edwin Muir had written that diary entry, in the summer of 1939.

'I was born before the Industrial Revolution, and am now two hundred years old. But I have skipped about a hundred and fifty of them. I was really born in 1737, and till I was fourteen no time-accidents happened to me. Then in 1751 I set out from Orkney for Glasgow. When I arrived I found that it was not 1751 but 1901, and that a hundred and fifty years had been burned up in my two days' journey. But I myself was in 1751, and remained there for a long time. All my life since I have been trying to overhaul that invisible leeway. No wonder I am obsessed with Time. Every summer, during my two weeks' holiday, I travelled back that hundred and fifty years again. What a relief it was to get back to the pre-industrial world, and how much better everything was arranged there! And even in Glasgow I could make little excursions into it on Saturday afternoon and Sunday by taking a walk into the country. On these walks I often met other Glasgow people doing the same thing. They thought they were "nature-lovers", but what really

drew them into the country was a . . . memory of a protective order which had existed before the modern chaos came upon us.'

Walking home with Inga, a pearl of a berry trundling about my palm, those words have been filling me up.

When I got home, I found my husband playing guitar on the floor with his back resting against the sofa. I put a huckleberry in his mouth and sat beside him. He leaned over and kissed my cheek. I said I would like berry picking to be my life. He said I would not like that. He said, 'An activity is fun because it's not your whole life; if it was your entire existence then it would no longer be so.'

I patted the dog resting beside us and said that was not true. 'Life could get worse for a species. For example this dog was once a wolf. Now she is inside a damp flat. And all her frustrations at her situation come out as barks and straining.'

'She gets out a lot,' he said.

'Only on a leash,' I replied. The dogs are on leashes. The toddlers are on leashes. I think we must be lonely, to have a dog. Pets are for the lonely. They were always making surrogate families out of the local wildlife in the past. In the 1850s, a journalist from *California Life* paid some local miners a visit. They were the first rugged individualists. But they did not seem so rugged. One man had a pet coon for a companion. Another had a California lion. One man had a whole pet family who accompanied him wherever he went. His children were a bay horse, two dogs, two sheep, and two goats. That journalist thought these animals seemed to be very mean substitutes for families at home, but 'poor fellows,' he said, 'what better could they do?'

I stroked the puppy's legs and said how free she could have been in the past, running about fields all day long. Eating leftover offal. Chasing lambs with the other animals.

'She is provided with constant warmth and food and shelter now,' he said, gently tucking my hair behind my ear.

'It takes a space as large as the British Isles just to feed all these dogs kibble.'

'If she was feral,' he replied, 'then from a young age she'd be giving birth to litter after litter of puppies. In no time her teats would be painfully scraping across the rocks. She'd be sore with infections. Do you think your woman's life in the past would have been so different?'

'Her heart would know the sea.'

'You think you want a time when families lurched from one house to the next. When each laird held the fates of many lives by thin threads. Do you fancy your chances? In a smoke-filled hut stirring pots?'

'Yes.'

'The man of your house would be your misery, and his mother.'

'His mother would of course be a cruel one!' I said, warming to the bleak image he was painting for me.

'And God would terrify you. You'd worry about your dead children eternally in Hell, you'd fear demons striking their infant heads with fiery clubs over some sin we'd now view as inconsequential. And all around you there'd be wet bristly dogs trundling in and out, black smoke, aching lungs. You'd be crunching grains day in day out. Dealing with rats—'

'I wouldn't be so fussed about rats then. I'd be different, tougher,' I said, resting my chin on my knees. 'Yes, I'd be used to it—sores and sickness. I'd have lice for pets. And if I made it to this age, well, there'd have been milk running all through and over me for years and years; I'd be bodily robust. Quite robust. Anyway, given the difficulties of my birth, it's quite clear that without modern hospital intervention I wouldn't have survived a day.'

'Then how can you—'

'My point isn't about me as an individual. Anyway I'm not interested in statistics about how people's life expectancy has improved exponentially. Those averages don't say a thing about lived experiences on the inside. There's nothing of value in my life that can be seen.'

'Your inner life would be a wreck. You could not see beauty in the ocean then. Carrying your husband on your back through freezing shallows. Dropping him into his boat. Baiting the lines with sheep wool and mussels. It was a hard life. And if and when he died? You'd get widows' rations from the community if you were lucky. Or maybe they'd just sink you.'

'They didn't really go in for that in the Hebrides.'

'Look,' he said, dropping my hair, 'you're not from the Hebrides and the water was not a friendly otter. The number of women in your bones who spent their nights watching storms battering the windows, their inner lives blacked out with pacing and humming, with running down to the shore at first light, searching for signs of a boat. You don't want that.'

I did want that. I did want the time before we started dipping sheep in arsenic. I did want the time before Formica and linoleum. If he was not around, I would not have to live here. I could rent a croft and have iron pots swinging from the ceiling.

Anyway it's not just me dreaming of gold. It's that Una Macdonald with her talk of mouth-music that's been spinning these gauzy thoughts in me.

In the nineteenth century she lived on South Uist; she told the folklorist Alexander Carmichael, 'At the summer shielings there might be a dozen or two dozen women and girls, with a sprinkling of men and boys, singing and dancing, carolling and prancing, upon the green grass under the shining light of the moon, the moonbeams shimmering—'

It was a total hooch-up with the clapping of the girls, she said. The women's singing reverberating in the rocks, combined with the surroundings, made up a picture that could be neither described nor forgotten.

A picture neither described nor forgotten!

But going up to the high hills every summer was not done for fun, was it.

Moving the animals up and down through the seasons has never been done for fun. Transhumance occurs where grazing ground is poor.

And there must have been bad years. Years when the air was fused with a malevolence bringing hunger and sickness to all.

I need stories of those terrible soaked summers, which did exist, *Una*.
Those terrible shieling years when the fruit-and-fire-demanding spirits could not be appeased
I need to keep in mind
When the hill spirits acted appallingly
And no amount of heather stuffed up jackets could keep the old ones warm
And hands and grain sacks bloomed blue into autumn.
I do need to set my mind on those hardships.

Oh but Una, you would have known. The blaeberries on the mountainsides. When you go pressing them between your teeth and tongue, they're bursting like stars.

Rats

September 21

I suppose the problem with my husband's and my divergent ideas of the past is down to us stumbling into some kind of dark wardrobe. In the angled shadows, we've been picking up items fallen from hangers. We've been running the fabrics blindly through our fingers in order to guess at their meaning. Obviously he's been holding hairshirt after hairshirt—items rough and bristling—and so he thinks the past was all misery. I'm holding gossamer.

I keep telling him that I know his items exist. I'm just saying a hairshirt cannot bleed nipples if silk is shielding the skin. A rough goat hair tankard might in fact be a perfectly lovely thing to wear so long as one has something soft flowing beneath it. There's no sensation of bristling then, there's no jabbing and jostling in an outfit like that. There's secret gold all day long. That's all I'm saying.

Of course in his mind the hairshirt goes on first. And I know the fine, filmy nature of my golden item can't make a mote of difference then. A wiry vest worn with a translucent robe on top, that's a filthy state to be caught out in. And well, he may be right. He may well be right. The external world may well come before the internal.

This week I've been drawing rats on sheets of paper so I can understand what the past was really like.

Pictures of rats I know I need. I've been painting them with walnut ink till they're writhing; their eyes like pins, they're pissing on blankets. I've been drawing them, and virulent fleas and flechs and weevils. And ravens dipping their beaks into the eyes of the newborn lambs. And rats, and more and more and more rats gushing forth, gnawing at dropped eyeballs. Large warm ones with scaled tails, they're coiling round the bedposts. Rats wet and brown and soaked, they're scurrying onto coasts from Scandi-boats.

Now he's coming in from work, he's looking at the drawings lining the skirting boards. He's taking off his sweater as I explain myself. He's opening his arms. He's saying how lucky I am, now I'm living in the world's largest rat-free land mass.

I'm saying that's the best thing about this sorry province.

His arms are slumping down by his sides now.

I always do take it too far now. It's just that I'm so tired.

Gold

September 23

A great storm came in from the Arctic at the beginning of the week. Town apples thundered into slumpen mushrooms. Now a north wind is cutting into the schoolchildren's cheeks.

These mountain seasons, I should be used to them but I'm not at all. I still imagine frosts don't begin until late November.

What to do now? I suppose there are universal actions beyond foraging that I could perform in order to feel my ancestors living again through me. There is always kissing and pissing. Well, he's at work all day and I don't feel like kissing an orange. Still, I can take my pisses outside. I can do that. I cannot milk a cow or skin a bird or weave a hat or dress or sock, but this week I've been doing all of my pissing outside to see if I like it.

I do like it.

It's quite the feeling, creating warm gold streams among the rosehips.

At the same time, it's quite the palaver. After all, I only have one very long skirt to go out in. It's a drifting sort of skirt in the ideal shade of tangerine. Actually it's quite brown and mucky now I've been dragging it through the woods each morning and afternoon, and then again before dark. There are thorns in it now, and the hem is swollen with damp.

It's always the same way. After drinking two or three cups of tea, on standing I'll feel a sudden pressure arcing beneath my stomach. I'll run to the hallway and dig out my boots from beneath the coats. I'll pull them on, my jumpers and gloves, then I'll swing through the door and get on the bike and pedal very fast. Yet I always do leave things too late; I always do, and though the saddle acts as a sort of corset relieving pressure from my bladder while I'm pedalling, as soon as I'm off the bike and in the bushes a bit of pee comes out. No more than a slight moistening. Still, I've had to stop wearing pants, and I've begun to wonder if peeing outside nowadays isn't just a bit of a faff. From start to finish it just hasn't felt worth it, given that there's a perfectly serviceable bathroom three steps from the kitchen.

Now I'm back to sitting alone on the toilet with the shampoo bottle for company. And though it's not a joy, it's more convenient. And when it comes down to it, I know I'm full of shit. My self, so used to ease, rarely chooses beauty when pressed.

Hirta

September 25

I don't like my rat pictures. I've replaced them with photos from a book about Hebridean life. Above the toaster now I'm looking at an old woman milking a cow. Even the cow looks startled by the wind.

I've filleted images of a woman with her sheep.

Of a woman holding her wool-ball.

I want a sheep.
I want a wool-ball.

These pictures aren't what I need.

What I need are pictures of those horrible limpet-sick winters,
The exciseman bent on the path,
The mass of filthy sea lace rising towards the door

Infants in their graves,
And the beds so cold

The cow's legs buckle as he goes slicing at her throat
He brings hot blood to our moontime girls
For them, I stir pulp into oats.

What was she doing in Scotland, the woman who took these images? Margaret Fay Shaw was born in 1903 to a wealthy steel family outside Pittsburgh. Orphaned at a young age, her aunts didn't know what to do with one as wild as her. When Margaret was a teenager, she was sent across the Atlantic to a boarding school near Gourock.

One day, in the school's back garden, a Traveller in an old army coat was playing the pipes. Margaret thought, 'I'm going to talk to him.' Her teachers wouldn't let her, but I think she rushed out anyway. If I'm to guess why this story sticks with me, it's that she would have understood the British class system she'd been thrust into. Posh girls like her were at one end; Travellers were at the other. Travellers were seen as particularly nasty sort of vermin—to the point where country women eschewed brambles because of who left their washing out to dry on the bushes.

Margaret Fay Shaw would have been well aware, just from the disapproving tone of her teachers, that girls like her weren't meant to go out meeting old pipers. I think what was happening was this—she had a feeling for music. So when she heard him play, it didn't matter who he was. She heard beauty. And this was a gift, for it allowed her to see through the narrowness of class into the truth of art—which springs from infinite sources. And this opened up all kinds of possibilities for her.

After boarding school, Shaw received classical music training in New York City. She waitressed till she had enough money to sail back to Britain. Then she bought a cheap bike in Oxford, and with a pair of friends pedalled north from England across the Scottish border. On reaching the Western Isles, the roads grew quiet; manes of grass swished up their centres.

The girls went to crofts.
They talked with the folk.
They listened to their songs.
Margaret didn't want to stop listening.

In 1929, she moved in with a pair of elderly sisters. Mairi and Peigi MacRae lived on South Uist. They wore their hair in crowns of silver. They grew their own food and knitted their own outfits. And now they had a boarder.

Margaret learned the Gaelic language from Mairi and Peigi, and many songs.
When she could, she went off to various islands. She took ferries out to Arran, to Mingulay.

On the isle of Skye she saw an open-air church service take place in a field. There were carts and ponies everywhere, and I feel it must have made quite the impression on her.

If I am writing about it now, I suppose her written version of the scene made quite an impression on me. All those folk being outdoors together, that's what I like.

Margaret's teeth were large and straight. She was confident—she must have been, to go loosening people into sharing their songs all over the place.

Wherever she went, Margaret took photos. For a while she had no tripod—they were heavy and expensive. Instead she would ask someone to crouch on all fours so she could balance her heavy Graflex camera on their back.

In the frame would be moonrises, mountains, marram grass. But never without the people centred in frame—never without the people who were part of the place.

She photographed people cutting hay.

She photographed a woman holding a fish above a bunch of cats.

The people made pets of everything, she said. So did she.

Over the following decades in Scotland she photographed her dozing kittens, her pet lambs, her little dogs, her cows.

Margaret was one of very few people going about listening to and recording the old songs. Those songs crooned for centuries while rocking a cradle or working the spinning wheel; they were vanishing.

And though it was not easy—for much of the singing she heard was not in a major or minor key, but in the half-notes in between—she was able to note down oral compositions thanks to her music training. 'An ember was dying,' her poet-friend Fred T. Gillies said. 'She blew on it and brought it to life.'

Margaret Fay Shaw recorded a world that she loved. There are moments she witnessed that are still alive. They're lying beneath my hands now as I touch these reproduced images.

When she sailed out to St Kilda in the summer of 1930, what did Margaret notice? Those tuggy dogs tumbling about the crystalled shore. Women in trimmed velvet skirts holding knitted socks and blown eggs for sale.

Did she talk to them,
Those bird-women who crawled the sea stacks?

Those women would reach their hands into shady burrows all summer,
And find warm bodies shaking beneath charcoal feathers
A puffling
A meal.

Maybe she saw the women digging in the communal garden while they imitated the skirl of seabirds flying over—

Inn ala oro i, o inn al ala;
  Inn ala oro i, uru ru-i uru ru-i
    Inn ala oro i, o inn al ala

Given her nature, it likely was not long before she was chatting with them.

Perhaps she was asking a little about their brooches—they'd hammer them from coins washed ashore from shipwrecks.

Suppose she was striding up and down the hill, witnessing women sitting in the grass, their breaths huffing on errant stems as they rolled white, feathery booties up their legs. They'd slit the long necks of gannets, then flip them inside out, so feathers lay warm against cold calf muscles.

And the men.
She'd have talked with them.
She'd have looked at their feet.
How could you not?
Those toes permanently splayed.
Those feet flat and huge because, in summer, they'd be resting the entirety of their body weight on their tippy-toes as they crept up wet rocks, snaring fulmars with horsehair ropes.

Visitors would always be trying to get a comparison photo of their own feet beside them.

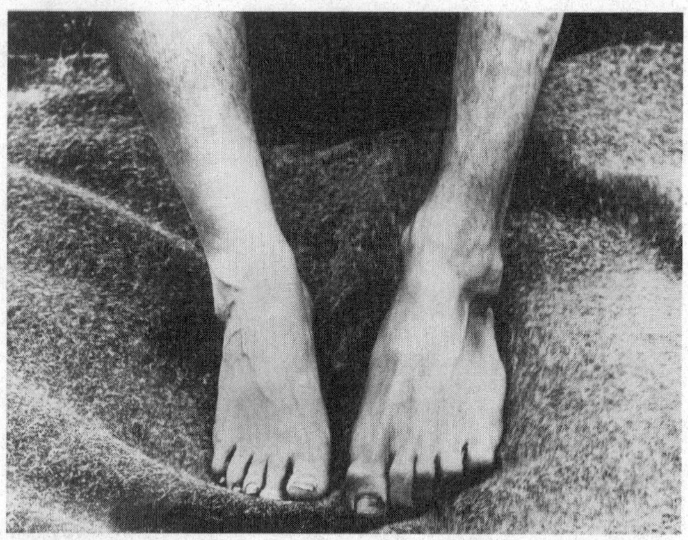

Of course Margaret Fay Shaw was not the first outsider to go to the island. Holidaymakers had been coming in for a peep since the Victorian days. St Kilda had been exciting people on steamers for half a century. What were the tourists thinking? The usual, most likely.

So untouched and sublime a place!

Some visitors were polite and gave the children sweets. Others were rude and drunk and threw their confectionery at the people's feet.

And what does that do to a person's self-worth and sense of dignity?

Things had been going badly for the islanders for some time. More and more of the young were upping sticks for the mainland, for Australia, for Canada. What babies were being born were dying too often from tetanus infantum.

There comes a point when an isolated population can no longer remain viable. St Kilda had reached that point. The community was struggling to feed itself.

The year Margaret Fay Shaw visited was the year all thirty-six remaining St Kildans voted collectively to leave the island.

On 10 May 1930, they wrote to the Right Hon. Sir W. Adamson mp, Secretary of State for Scotland, Westminster—

'We the undersigned the natives of St Kilda, hereby respectfully pray and petition H.M. Government to assist us all to leave the island this year and to find homes and occupation for us on the mainland.

'The reason why assistance is necessary is that for many years Saint Kilda has not been self-supporting, and with facilities to better our position, we are therefore without the means to pay for the costs of removing ourselves and furniture elsewhere. We do not ask to be settled together as a separate community, but in the meantime we would collectively be very grateful for assistance, and transference elsewhere, where there would be a better opportunity of securing our livelihood.'

The evacuation took place after much parliamentary discussion. There was concern about the optics of providing help to one group at a time when high unemployment rates were impacting voters everywhere.

A few months later though, the St Kildans were engaged in their long goodbye.

Certainly the birds rejoiced.

August 29, 1930, St Kilda

Sheena and Margaret and Ingrid and Catherine are bending their heads in a steely line before the sailors have even pulled the chains from the harbour. A haar goes swirling over land and shattered sea.

Five thousand continuous years of human habitation, of spinning and weaving, are now all over.

O al ala.

Neil watches the mist enclose the island as the boat chugs away from the shore.

He watches the dogs bobbing silently in the water. When he can no longer look, he feels for his wife's hands tucked neatly in her skirt folds.

He leans in, touches her cheek. *Just me and you,* he says. *Just me and you,* Mary Ann whispers back.

October 28, 1930, Loch Carron

Neil had few complaints about life on the mainland at first, for he and Mary Ann had been placed far from his father as requested. And the lads at the forestry were alright, aye they were good lads he was working with. The money was okay too. He couldn't really say anything against that. It was just that before, he and Sandy and Tom would be cutting and drying the peat together. There was a week to cut and cast, a week of Sandy making them cry with laughter, then there was enough peat to last them all a year.

Now it was two miles around the hill to Stromeferry to purchase coal. And the coal was lonely to carry on his back, and the cost was cutting into every coin he had.

Still, he liked the purple moors alright. When they'd arrived the colour spread across the hills was beyond belief. All that shimmery heather. And silver trees by the stream. *Silver birch*, the forestry manager had said, on seeing Mary Ann staring at them. The pair had burst out laughing then. Silver birch! They'd never heard of such a thing. They'd never seen a tree.

On that first night, Neil's heart had filled with hope watching Mary Ann set out her coat and good blanket on the chairs. He felt that, with each careful placement, she was claiming this new life as theirs.

They'd lain on the floor that night and looked up at the walls. The bottom of the wallpaper was green and plain, then rows of yellow roses climbed up through diamonds to the ceiling. They felt they were in a meadow, looking up then.

Of course there were small problems from the off. The walls of the house were damp, causing black specks in the wallpaper. But a few weeks with the fire going would see to that. She'd be quite busy setting this place to rights, she joked, *no time to make the tea.*

He worried about Mary Ann being in the house by herself all day. Yet she promised there was much for her to like. *This might even be a good place to try again for a child*, she'd said, tentatively, in those first days.

Mary Ann had sounded, yes, *happy* as she rose in the mornings. As she squatted by the fire while he dozed before work, he'd hear her intone,

I am kindling my fire this morning
In presence of the holy angels of heaven,
Without malice, without jealousy, without envy,
Without fear, without terror of any one under the sun,
But the Son of God to shield me.

He'd felt his mother with them then.

Those words,
Mother had chanted them every morning too.

Every morning

Togaidh mi mo theine an diugh,
An lathair athlean naomh nimh,
Gun ghnu, gun tnu, gun fharmad.
Gun gniomh, gun gheimeh roimh beach fun ghrelin,
Ach Naomh Mhac De da m' thearmad.

She'd packed him and Tom off with the sunrise as soon as they could walk.
Out they all went, all the children, to imitate the snipes and wrens and oystercatchers.
They whooped and cooed. They burbled and gurgled. At first that was all they could do.

Neil would come back crying because he couldn't sing. He couldn't praise the birds with his voice. Mother would kneel down then and wipe his cheeks and call him her little bird.

She'd take him alone to the cliffs. Together they listened to the birdsong. *The chicks can't sing yet either*, she'd say. *But they'll get better. They're listening to everything around them. That's all it is. You just listen to their mummies and daddies. You'll sing too.*

Every day that summer, Neil listened.
It felt like forever until he could successfully call out,

Inn ala oro.

Mary Ann though, she'd sounded lovely from the off.

The morning after the storm had knocked out Sheena's door
Flocks of starlings rimmed the stones.
They shone like peat oil—

He and Sandy went out chasing them
Then Sally and Tom and John and Mary Ann came out running

Sandy had a go at imitation
If he did not sound like a slug schlooping about the grass

Sally went next
Sounded just like the steamer's dirge

Poor Tom sounded like a puffling bubbling in a hot pan

And John had never not sounded like his old daddy parping

Then Mary Ann looked up at the sky
Her mouth opened
And soon the starlings were singing back
They were really singing, all at once

Mary Ann's voice.
He felt it running down his throat

It's stayed there ever since.

November 7, 1930, Loch Carron

It had been a beautiful September, a mild October. The ulcers that had illed Neil on the island had gone. The backache from felling wood was new. But between them were joys and shared pleasures.

Walking back from the yard in the early evenings, he'd see Mary Ann resting her back against the frame of the open door.

When he reached her, she'd press her thumb against his eyelids, left then right. She'd brush flowerheads against his cheeks, his lips.

Bog cotton
Heather
Myrtle

She'd whisper their names.

Ceannbhán
Fraoch
Roideóg

But now it was November, and the flowers on the heath were all dead, and it was cold and wet, and in the darkness of the new season bleak images kept flashing before Neil's eyes.

Those dogs floating in the bay.
No use for them now, Father had said to the others.

He couldn't look at Sandy tying the stones on.
He couldn't watch them being dropped yelping into the water.

Father had noticed.
Of course he'd noticed.
Said *cheer up, it's not you who's drowning.*

Father. Father. Bastard father.

Sandy, Sandy, how was he? Sandy all jokes and charm, Sandy all legs and arms, Sandy quick as thunder, whipping his handkerchief around his thin neck like a dove collar, bearing down in perfect impersonation of Minister Mackay bellowing, *All of you for the sake of your souls you must go!*

Aye Mackay said they could evacuate quite easily, aye oh aye oh aye, it was *him* saying how positively *improved* their lives would be on the mainland. On and on he went, calling it *an opportunity*.

Sandy helping to string the stones around those poor beasts' necks, Sandy impersonating Nurse Barclay saying to the wee ones *jam for you jam for you and wee hen jam for you*. Well he laughed but he liked her a lot. Aye Nurse Barclay was a stellar one.

Sandy had begged her to join them on the boat as soon as she arrived on the island. He was all grovel and polish when he wanted to be, and he was right. Without her on board, they'd as likely be hit in the head with fish guts as get an ounce of sup off a Lewis trawlerman. What they needed was a *fine upstanding Glaswegian lady like herself*. And she'd come!

She took the trips out in that tiny rowboat well, even when the waves dashed them in the heads and rain nearly drowned them. When they reached a trawler, she'd hold on to the side and shout across the water, *Please give us some potatoes, because we have hardly anything to eat*. And so long as it was her doing the asking, potatoes they received.

Still.

Begging.

He couldn't believe they'd been reduced to begging.

Before agreeing to sign the letter addressed for Westminster, Neil had gone and asked Nurse Barclay for her opinion on the evacuation. She'd sat him down in her kitchen and made him a cup of tea. She'd looked awfully sorry as she said, *Between you and me and the deep blue sea, I think you are on your last legs.*

Stones in his gut, around his neck.

And now the frosts had come and the myrtle had sunk to pudding. And it was taking forever to come home through the seething bog, and the moon was but a dim shard, and his boots flapping into wet turf.

Well he could just sink right in.

Maybe he just should. Because with the cold, the rats had come. Rats were eating the glue behind the wallpaper and it was dark in the mornings and dark when he came back and his back was always aching and his hands were splintered and cut. And just what were the authorities thinking when they put them in a croft with no road?

Rats with their drenched whiskers and wet noses, rats too clever, what was he supposed to do with them? There hadn't been rats on the island. And the forestry lads' only suggestion was to get a puss. Well a cat could barely catch a guga; he wasn't wasting his time with one of those. His feet were damp all the time now and he was getting sick. And he was sorry. He was so so sorry. For he was twenty-eight and his frozen hands were turning into Grandfather's claws. He was twenty-eight and she was kissing his lids like they might not open again.

He was fine, he kept saying. But he wasn't, was he. And nor was she. Last night, when he'd entered the house, he'd found the wallpaper shredded all the way up to the chair heads.
Flames in his chest then.
Mary Ann what in the name, he'd roared.

I left the roses, she replied.

It was true. She'd left the blooms in their diamonds untouched.
God.
God but God.
A red pool was running from one of the spots where she'd knifed the wallpaper loose.

The rats, she said.
Love, he said, guiding her sobbing onto the bed.
Sing me the one to the geese, he'd said.
She looked at him with swollen eyes,
Then turned around on her side.

Love, he said, wiping his eyes.
Love please, he said.
He ran his hand around her thigh.

She scratched his wrist and went over to the fire.

That night he dreamed they were walking along a cliff edge. They were dodging giant anemones while lightning struck the ground around them. Were they meant to stand together or apart? He couldn't remember. He just didn't know.

When he awoke, she was kindling the fire in silence.
She said all night she'd imagined rats crawling on her. And with the cold coming, this was it. All winter they'd live with rats, wouldn't they?

Well he worried too. And he didn't know what they'd do if they got to her coat, if they started touching his hand cuts.

In the morning, they got ready for Minister Nell's service in silence.

They walked along the shoreline in the gloaming.

He remembered the birds at home. The snares being set, the houses all feathered in whiteness. Feathers on the shawls of Sheena and Margaret and Ingrid and Catherine, smiling themselves to youth. And Mary Ann in the grass beside him. And Sandy batting his eyelashes like gull wings.

He needed them,
All of them.
He called out then,

Inn a la rooooooooooooo

And then he heard,
Oh joyous sound,
Mary Ann calling back,

Innnn allllllla roooooooooo

You and me, he said, when she'd caught up with him.

By the time they reached the village, everyone was already in the kirk. Mary Ann tugged his sleeve and hastened them through the doors. As soon as they sat down, Neil felt the bile in him rising. It was seeing the minister's house that soured him. The pale sun shining on the windows. And that big plum tree blooming with robins. Why did he get to have such a lovely house? Why did he get to have electric lights? Why was he not living on a squirming moor with rats trundling in and out?

That prig on a plinth. Those words slithering through his murky teeth, the whole of Stromeferry bobbing their heads in return.

This minister, talking of wrath and sin,
No
No
No terror came from God's presence.
Hell was coming from Man.
From the Big Men in Westminster,
On the altar and in the home.
Heaven was in everything else.

Aye, and he knew where this sermon was going. This minister talking of the importance of charity, of giving—oh aye this talk was heading straight towards the collection bowl, was heading straight towards the minister's lawn upkeep.

He just wasn't going to have it.
Neil needed charity.
Neil needed shoes.
Neil needed an end to rats and splinters and bogs and coals and her endless bloody bannocks and he was going to write to

the government about it—he wasn't going to have it. They had another thing coming if they thought they could treat him like this.

The skin under Neil's nails was arcing white now,
Heat was pulsing through him now.
What Neil needed now, right now,
Was to press his thumbs very hard against this pew,
Until he felt teeth splintering,
Stones melting,
The rising up of boulders,
Spinning apart,
Then silvering into smithereens,
Into sand.

It was big news that the St Kildans were leaving their only home. It was in all the newspapers. Plenty, on reading, would have clucked *poor souls, poor loves, poor ducks*. Others were most definitely stomping their slippered feet upon the egg-toast floor and saying *not my money, not my taxes*.

Of course, others' stockinged feet were tapping their new linoleum like piano pedals,
Oh to live on that moonlit island! Oh just imagine!

The romantics of the 1930s were *of course* dreaming of pushing the walls out. They were pushing the walls out and the pavements and the hedgerows till they were on that heavenly island.

Imagine living there. No buses, no bosses. Life would be simple then. With a fishing net to catch their tea. And a little stone house. *Oh to live on an island like a luminous green iceberg!*

The island's laird, Sir Reginald MacLeod, soon began receiving requests from members of the British public asking if they might be given permission to move to St Kilda (it is perhaps for the best that their requests were declined).

It's funny. I always thought the desire for a peaceful life was a relatively new thing. Such romantic follies, I imagined, began around the time Ben Fogle and four thousand others applied to be on the BBC reality tv show *Castaway* in the run-up to the new millennium.

Thirty-six men, women and children were selected to live on the island of Taransay for a year.
There was an outbreak of flu and six left early.
Another five set up their own camp and refused to participate in

filming (on their patch of island they raised a flag of their own making).
Some smuggled mobile phones onto the island.

Grey clouds loosened *constantly* on the participants' heads.
It was, in many ways, a disaster.

In Margaret Fay Shaw's photos—of a woman beside a beached whale bone, of a girl holding a thread—there is often another presence contained within the frame.

In a corner of so many of her photographs
There is the shadow of Margaret
A shadow but unmistakably her.

There is her hat and her shoulder
Her hat and shoulder and chest
Her hat and shoulder and chest and camera
There she is.

She was too adept a photographer to go leaving her shadows in the frame without there being a reason. What was she trying to say with each dusky slip?

Her shadow in these photos, my fingers keep outlining.
Why is that?

These people being photographed, they're not alone.

This person who is doing the photographing,

Nor's she.

If this is the value I am projecting on these spectres, then I must think there is value in togetherness.

I must need more than Inga and my husband.
He's away for work this week, and I've been messaging a stranger online. Tomorrow we're meeting in the woods.

Autumn

Clara

October 15

Though my husband prefers the bedroom window closed, I like it open in summer and through much of winter. I like hearing the sounds from the small patch of woods at the back of the flat. The crows ribbiting on the hill, the children walking around the surrounding flats and trailers. It's just the sounds of the road at the front of the house that send my teeth ringing. It's the sounds of the traffic, it's the highway at the bottom of the path, it's the trains. It's as loud as a port here, with the slopes acting as sound-mirrors.

When I talked to Inga about it, she said that if I wanted to accept the sounds of the train, then maybe I could try to give myself some cheap exposure therapy by sitting very close to the tracks one day. If I did that, then the train from my bedroom would seem distant by comparison.

I liked that idea, so after breakfast this morning, I spent the rest of the day sitting on the path by the railway line. The aspen leaves were trembling like mangoes and the mountains were fresh with night snow and looking at the trees with train sounds in my ears was like looking at a flower while eating a bag of dirt.

There is a cost to hearing these sounds. Birds age faster in noisy areas and I don't see why the same wouldn't hold true for us.

As a reaction to noise pollution, our IQ lowers, more stress hormones show in our bloodstream, and we do more poorly in performance tests.

There's one study that says we continue to detect noises even while sleeping. Those little detections lift us out of deeper, more restorative cycles of sleep into shallower, less restorative ones. Scientists think our ancient brains can't help but transform those horns and honks into growls and paws moving in our direction. Naturally we wake up knackered.

I'm not naturally adept at loving the sounds of the train, but there must be someone who loves the sounds of action, of progress, of people.

Clara could love those sounds.

Yes.

Clara de Lune may not have loved the country where nothing stirred but insects. She did not love nibbling at dry dumplings and fighting with her brothers. But since leaving the farm, she has been so happy in the city. Heading down pendulous alleyways and stopping for hot chestnuts, ducking beneath vaulted doors and ordering ales, every free hour here in the city has been new and special. Every careening sound has suggested fresh excitements around the bend.

Each day during her lunch break, Clara places her order at the bakery, then sits on the bench outside the house of the piano player.

It is beautiful to be sitting there.

Eating a penny bun, swigging on ginger beer, smiling to herself as she listens to *Deux arabesques* and *Syrinx* being played, Clara feels like she made the right decision to move.

After lunch, for six more hours she gets paid to stand in front of a mirrored counter. She watches men fondle silk hats while Mr. Bergamasque sits behind his desk and chows down peanuts. In these instances, she begins to feel less sure about her decision to have come here.

But there are worse jobs.

Mr. Bergamasque left the shop tonight at 6:20 pm. Clara swept the day's dust beneath the counter. She rubbed beetroot juice on her lips and cheeks, and by 6:27 pm she was running down to the concert hall.

Mar was already in the lobby waiting for her. She touched the silver comb in Clara's hair then said, 'We'd better hurry, it's already packed!'

They took the stairs two at a time to the top of the hall. An usher guided them into their stall. The wallpaper looked like the insides of a children's book. There were elephants and camels, fruits and flowers were reaching far, far up past the golden boxes to the ceilings. In the box nearest them sat a lone woman sleeping. Her quilt had slipped from her shoulders towards her lap. Eleven men in suits came on stage. They sat in chairs beside wooden boxes inlaid with horns. Clara whispered, 'What are those?' Mar shrugged, then the composer walked on. His coattails were like brown wings. Clara took an immediate dislike to him. He was bowing to the crowd. The lights were dimming. He was announcing, 'The Awakening of the City!'

The musicians brought their hands towards the boxes and began winding cranks.

Huge sounds filled the air
Tomb tomb tomb went one box
From another came big loud slaps
There were grotesque shrieks
Horrendous puffs
Vilest whistles

A purple feeling was surging through the crowd. Audience members were tugging at their cloaks. The woman in the box nearest them was suddenly up, clutching her wig and shrieking at the stage. Clara's fingers were touching a wet corner of her pamphlet; she realised then she must have been nibbling the paper. It was the violence of the music that made her want to bite things. Then Mar was pulling on her sleeve, and Clara was following her down the skidding-aisles.

She took one last look back at the stage—a musician's face was meeting a flying cane. The composer was boxing an audience member.

Outside in the plaza with the crowds, Clara coughed up black dust. She watched it glitter in her hanky. Then Mar was pulling again and they were running down twisting lanes, past teasing dogs, past women shaking rugs, past belching steam pipes, past trams and palace stables, and their lungs hurt, it really hurt to breathe in the dark air.

At home, Mar went to the kitchen and put on a pot of water. She sat on the stool and nestled her forehead in her palm. 'Next time,' she said, 'I'll just get you a vase.' Clara flicked her on the arm and said no it had been good. 'We're not in the country now are we,' she said, remembering the violence of the music, and suddenly she felt besieged with happiness. *Besieged*.

In her room, Clara changed into her sleep trousers and shirt. She propped herself up against the bed rail and opened her pamphlet from the concert. The whole thing was a manifesto from the composer Luigi Russolo. He said it was time to abandon the classical music of the past and embrace the future, the future of noise—of industry, the machine. She had never read words like it. He had written, 'We must break at all costs from this restrictive circle of pure sounds and conquer the infinite variety of noise-sounds.' He said he belonged to a Milano artists' collective. He said, 'We enjoy creating mental orchestrations of the crashing down of metal shop blinds, slamming doors, the hubbub and shuffling of crowds, the variety of din, from stations, railways, iron foundries spinning wheels, printing works, electric power stations and underground railways.

'For years, Beethoven and Wagner have deliciously shaken our hearts. Now we are fed up with them. This is why we get infinitely more pleasure imagining combinations of the sounds of trolleys, autos and other vehicles, and loud crowds, than listening once more, for instance, to the heroic or pastoral symphonies.

'It is hardly possible to consider the enormous mobilisation of energy that a modern orchestra represents without concluding that the acoustic results are pitiful. Is there anything more ridiculous in the world than twenty men slaving to increase the plaintive meowing of violins?

'POUAH! Let's get out quickly, for I can't repress much longer the intense desire to create a true musical reality finally by distributing big loud slaps right and left, stepping and pushing over violins and pianos, bassoons and moaning organs! Let's go out!

'Let's walk together through a great modern capital, with the ear more attentive than the eye, and we will vary the pleasures of our sensibilities by distinguishing among the gurglings of water, air, and gas inside metallic pipes, the rumblings and ramblings of engines breathing with obvious animal spirits, the rising and falling of pistons, the stridency of mechanical saws, the loud jumping of trolleys on their rails, the snapping of whips, the whipping of flags. We will have fun imagining our orchestration of department stores' sliding doors, the hubbub of the crowds, the different roars of railroad stations, iron foundries, textile mills, printing houses, power plants, and subways.

'Let's go out!

'Noise accompanies every manifestation of our life. Noise is familiar to us. Noise has the power to bring us back to life. On the other hand, sound, foreign to life, always a musical, outside thing, an occasional element, has come to strike our ears no more than an overly familiar face does our eye.

'To convince you of the surprising variety of noises, I will mention thunder, wind, cascades, rivers, streams, leaves, a horse trotting away, the starts and jumps of a carriage on the pavement, the white solemn breathing of a city at night, all the noises made by feline and domestic animals and all those man's mouth can make without talking or singing.

'Such joy is yours o my people to sense see ear scent drink everything everything everything taratatatatata.'

Clara opened the window. The soot on the buildings shimmered under the street lights." Voices and horses and crackling whips could be heard ringing across the avenue. She loved the city, its noises and its dirt, its music and cream cakes and swarthy men who deliciously pumped their arms at her outside the shops. Such gorgeousness did not fruit silently in the night. There was no civilised beauty without civilised ugliness, why pretend otherwise? Without these noises, pouah, life would be what—insects and flour? The shrugging of cargo ships, the scraping of instrument cases, the cranking of machines created all that she loved. Let's go out!

If she were being honest though, she was getting a headache from having the window open. Her head certainly was hurting from the sounds of the yodelling night-boys. If she were to tell the truth, her head was pounding. Just for a moment, she needed a pause from rumbling omnibuses, from shrieks and meows.

In truth, just for a moment, she needed those ear plugs, glistening on her bedside table like pearls.

It turns out I cannot quite imagine a character who loves sounds just as they are. Yet there are others, after Russolo, who tried transforming noise into sound.

There's John Cage who—between composing silent songs and picking mushrooms—spent time in his Sixth Avenue loft listening to the sounds of the traffic far below. He never dreamed of getting double-glazing in. He said he loved all sounds, just as they were. Of course, on first moving into that noisy apartment, he was a bit worried about not being able to sleep.

But he soon learned to transpose sounds into images so they would enter his dreams as visuals that would not wake him. With practice, for Cage, a burglar alarm lasting several hours came to resemble a Brâncuşi sculpture.

I think I'd better learn how to lucid-dream like that. A lucid dream typically begins with the hands. You look at your hands all through the day—as you pick up a stone, as you pick up a leaf. You look at your hands that stretch out in octaves. You look at your knuckles and your ring. And then in your dreams, you are looking at your hands again. They're your hands, but they're also dream hands. And you'll know this because you have sixteen fingers. Because your hands are a translucent blur. Because there are pink tails coiled round your wrists and your fingernails are drifting into the ceiling. You really know you are in a dream then. And you can now work on spinning those sounds into bronze.

Yet how can I dream when I don't know how to sleep? When I've not slept I feel all my blood is going to my skull instead of my eyes. And every interaction—with the kitchen cupboards, with others—feels adversarial. I do wonder if I'd be less hateful if I lived in an old garden cottage amid bluebottles. After all, a lack of sleep does not make me feel furious when I'm outside camping. Lying awake while the forest animals are dozing, I feel the night pulsing with unfathomable beauty until morning. Rising stiff-backed from the tent, curling sleepless towards my teacup, I feel so beautifully skinned, my tears become mixed with laughter—for the whole sadness and beauty of life, on such mornings, seems to be revealed.

It's here in the flat, where I'm so easily warmed and fed that I hardly think about the miracle of electricity, where things go wrong. I sit by my kettle and my oven and desire a more beautiful environment than this one—a place with paned windows then trees. Biscuits not too sweet. A cloak nicer than my own one. Yes through the static indoor nights, the stains are entering and the train is entering and I have no sense of the world beyond myself. I'm at the centre of my thoughts and the train is at the centre of my thoughts and the train symbolises capital, and the feeling it produces in me at night is of not having enough—of being on the wrong side of the Freooooo Fronnnnnnng tracks that say with every clunking wheel—

Youuuure Poooooooor
Youuuure Poooooooor
Youuuureeeeee Poooooooooooooor

Of course I care about that. I was raised on the meanest and most divided isle in history; I do care. But I'd like to start caring about other things. I'd like to love more.

Sei

October 20

Colder now. The boulders in the creek have formed glassy domes of ice. Snow's falling on spiderwebs and it's past time to harvest, cut the hay, move the hay *swish*. Of course, I don't harvest hay. I do kitten work.

Until late afternoon, I edit stories about kittens for whom good or cute things have happened. They might have enjoyed their first-ever day playing in snow with all their kitten friends. Or a clever one with ginger stripes has learned how to open a door handle, and now all his cat friends are entering the human house so easily. Look at their swishy tails as they wander into the kitchen. I'm glad the videographer has set these escapades to a jaunty soundtrack. This video will surely do well once it's been posted.

How easily the time passes doing this work; certainly this is the best gig I've had. Not once has my boss asked how my weekend was. She has not asked to speak on a video call in nine months.

It's just that, after I've closed my tabs, the outside world no longer looks as fresh and inviting. Every afternoon, autumn collapses beneath winter's paws.

I'm often a bit gutted about missing the morning light.

I'm not the first one.

A young man living in 1950s New Jersey found his job meaningless, for he worked in the world of artificial flavouring. But once his work was over in the evenings, he felt that at least he could go out in the countryside and take photos of the things he loved—trees, water, light. He felt glad, doing this.

One evening after work, he was on a date. He showed the woman sitting across from him a few of his pictures over dinner. They touched a space inside her. Not a peaceful one. She was so angry with him. She said, 'Why are you showing me these hateful images?'

He was so surprised! He was capturing serene subjects, how could they be hateful? Then he realised the residual effects of his job were being reflected in every image. A stream appeared torrid and seemed to bellow forth with his own frustrations.

The photographer's emotional state will enter the viewer, he realised, so the artist must be careful with the emotions they share.

Daido Loori decided he wanted to invoke a peaceful feeling in others. To do that, he went out and deliberately tried to face his emotions. He photographed all his tiny furies snap, snap, snap, snap, snap, he snapped the rivers and he snapped the trees.

Eventually he left his job and became a Buddhist monk. He'd take groups of photographers out into nature. He'd encourage them to explore landscapes without expectations. When they found a subject, he said they would feel a connection. If that connection faded as they moved away or intensified as they came closer, they were to sit with their subject for a while, letting their presence be acknowledged. Intuition would guide them to the perfect moment to press the shutter.

This evening I've been trying to photograph my frustrations as they arise. I've been taking photos of the waxwings stripping the last of the rowan berries from the trees. These rusty-cheeked priests with juice-stained beaks have been plunging into fermenting fruits so fervently, I think they're getting drunk on them. They're lurching in the dusk. I can feel it. Winter is really coming in now.

It's good to photograph it. The frozen sky, the deer, the crows shining like bin bags, the leaves shaking like animals. The tree roots, the trucks, the trains, the trains, the trains.

Back inside the flat, I take off my boots and switch on the kettle. While waiting for the water to crackle, I photograph the broom's black hairs, the insides of the bin, the peach mould swinging from the bathroom ceiling.

Looking through the photo viewer, I realise these photos from inside and outside are the best I've ever taken.

Of course I am not the first woman to try to face what she despises. Sei Shōnagon was lady-in-waiting to a Japanese empress a thousand years ago. She wrote all her hates down in her diary.
All those things she found horrid and filthy then produce recognition and delight in me now.
What did she write of?

The damp little feet of flies when they land on your face,
Slugs,
Hair in an inkstone,
Hairless baby mice tumbled out of the nest,
Fleas,

The soft wind of a mosquito's tiny wings, just as you're trying to go to sleep,
Anyone less than attractive waking from a nap with a face all greasy and bloated—

Sei Shōnagon thought that herons were, and are, horrible.

She thought a suddenly snapped comb was, and is, startling and disconcerting.

And what else—
Exceptionally good-natured people are awful.
And so is the top of a broom used to sweep a shabby floor.
And so are people who don't close a door they've opened to go in or out.
And so is the heart of a man.

In her rarefied world of priests and oxen and palanquins, she wrote lists. Sitting behind a royal screen, in the coal dark she was writing down horrible things—

The inside of a cat's ear,
A chorus of dogs howling on and on.

As she sat by the oil lamp, she wrote of Things That Give an Unclean Feeling. She was screaming into a pillow with a pen. With murky daylight filtering through the blinds, she was writing, 'the blossom of the pear tree is the most prosaic, vulgar thing in the world'. She felt that to be true. And now each word of hers is a fresh-cut crystal flower—ageless, blooming.

With her long hair hanging loose about her thighs, I bet it felt good to write Things That Give a Pathetic Impression—

Crows screeching at their roost.

Holding a fur brush with tender fingertips, dipping it in silken ink, I bet she loved writing of terrible things—

River deeps,
Violent monks,
Iron,
Clods.

I bet she was smiling, of course she was. As she wrote, her teeth were glistening carbon.

Gourd

October 27

This week, while the sky outside was white and falling in splinters, I read some of Sei Shōnagon's lists of lovely things. And sumptuous things and moving things and amusing things. She wrote of the elegant, adorable, splendid and rare, including—

The mandarin duck,
The mountain dove,
Very black horses with just a little white somewhere,
The magnificent way the crane's cry reaches the heavens,
Shaved ice with sweet syrup, served in a shiny new metal bowl,
A good pair of silver tweezers,
Ornamental swords,
A crystal rosary,
A snap-beetle—

And all moonlight is moving, wherever it may be.
And so is a feeling of snow in the freezing air.

A baby's face painted on a gourd is endearingly lovely.

Sparrows are lovely, especially young sparrows.
And so is absolutely anything tiny.

Searching out an old letter on a rainy day when time hangs heavy is beautiful.
A letter on fine green paper, tied to a sprig of willow is a wonder.

Women who have not a single exciting prospect in life, yet who believe they are happy, are scornful.

The ageing of mothers is something nobody notices.

I wasn't ready to read that.

I notice the ageing of my mother. I notice everything about her. I see her so little.

Winter

Beaver

November 22

November. The Black Month, the Dark Month, the winds suddenly sharp. It's Saturday and, while he's sleeping, I've gone alone to the beaver lodge at the top of the hill.

The beavers there are living in a mud and lumber lodge of their devising. Tangled in their shadowy home, their warm, wet bodies are steaming as they go slipping all over each other. All winter they're down there at the edge of the icy pond. Then at some point, teeth will go cutting cords in the vanilla dark. Milky kits will come bursting forth.

I'd like to sit nearer them. I'd at least like to sit on top of their lodge and look down their airhole. Amid weak bends of light, I might see many eye-gems staring back—how our hearts would startle! If I place my hand just slightly to the left of my breastbone and think of their red insides as mine, I can feel their chests rising and falling, for our resting heart rates are practically the same. They're practically the same and the frosted twigs lying across their airhole are moving as tenderly as a record needle; while I look it's moving with the beat of their breaths. With the beat of my breath. The beavers' wet breaths and bodies are rising as mist from the top of their lodge and I can see the shape of them.

In a video I saw recently, someone placed a canoe paddle down a beaver lodge. Those iron teeth made the wood disappear in no time. Red teeth can make anything disappear. It's a shame that guns are stronger than teeth. With guns my ancestors took their ancestors' castor glands for cake, so by rights those beavers should be skidding across the ice to rip out my elbows.

For centuries, beavers' teardrop-shaped castor glands were being preserved with fire-smoke and sent across to Europe, where they were utilised by kitchen cooks as a means of lending a sweet and musky aroma to saffron cake batters. Of course it wasn't just their castor glands that made them vulnerable when the Hudson's Bay Company arrived here. Beaver pelts made perfect, waterproof hats. And so for huge profits, bucketloads of them were being taken and turned into tricornes and

Wellingtons and Regents and D'orsays. In frightening numbers, those pelts were being pummelled and boiled and tugged into most ornate headgear, so that in 1787 alone, 139,509 beaver skins were exported from regions now known as Canada—along with 68,142 martens, 26,330 otters, 16,951 minks, 8,913 foxes, 17,109 bears, 102,656 deer, 140,346 raccoons, 9,816 elk, 9,687 wolves, and 125 seals.

If in that time you were rich, European, and without qualms you might purchase obscene amounts of ribbons and ill-gotten lace; you might find yourself purchasing all manner of corals and canes and macaron wigs, and tiny, painted wooden globes slipped into fish skin cases to amuse yourself with on long journeys.

Now don't all those things sound like something of a crime given their cost to humans and other animals? But people then bought them.

They bought so many hats. Even into the late 1920s, if you were a lady in Europe without some sort of covering on your head, it was akin to walking around naked in public, such a scandal were you creating.

One of the first women to question the status quo lived in Madrid. She was named Maruja Mallo. She was a surrealist artist. She painted black smoke drifting from a pot, a dove screeching into a cliff, a woman dressed as an angel, a woman riding a pig. In one painting the fairground has come to town and the priests are watching, a swan is watching. The hair of a woman is like waves on the ocean.

At some point Mallo began refusing to wear hats. She and some of her pals went by the collective name Las Sinsombrero, the Hatless Women. They pressed their faces against the windows of taverns they were prohibited from entering.

For a long time I thought Mallo, while out and about, wore a silver gas balloon with a tiny hat attached to her wrist. For some reason I thought she made this little balloon talk to strangers—maybe by the duck pond in Retiro? There beside the toy boats? I don't think that was the case though. I think she just said that was something she *could* do, if she felt like it.

Inviting negative attention. Scandalising the old ones. I wish I was more like her. It's true I had misgivings about my last giddy purchase from the off. If I'd gone and spontaneously found a desiccated cow on the plain, that would be different. But buying a pair of cow's shin bones online from a ranch on the prairie? Why did I do that? It cost twenty dollars just to have them delivered. I'd believed I would attach the pair of greasy bones to my boots with twine then slide about an icy grey pond. I'd been imagining skating in vague emulation of prehistoric Nordic hunters.

Instead I have a pair of bones seeping liquid from a cardboard box that I can't bring myself to open. The box is on the hallway floor. My husband says it's my responsibility to get rid of it.

I've been keening for lots of things recently. Dresses so soft and well sewn I could wear them to bed. Plaits and scarfs and bits of string. Naot boots. Quilted red Lobbens with blue laces. And a crescent of gold. A moon pendant for my chest. The moon looks like a piece of jewellery sliding up and down the sky, but I know it's not what's compelling me to shop. If it was, Galileo

Galilei would be known for decking himself in all sorts of tinsel. But he never was swathing himself in crimson silks or duckbill shoes or sable collars slung about the shoulders. He once wrote a 301-line poem specifically stating that he would *not* wear a long gown because of its impractical nature. Galileo was not interested in clothes. Galileo just liked stars.

The golden necklaces I'd like to order, that I'd like tingling and babbling inside the freight trucks coming to town, it's not the moon putting them in my online basket.

Many units in this apartment building show signs of people hoarding. In apartment after apartment, goat paths lie between stacked books and electronics; I've seen it's so at night. I've read that hoarding may stem from some primal instinct to preserve stores of food. We want to feel safe in our caves with all our bits and pieces to stroke and hold and trade and so we hoard. Especially in hard times, in times equivalent to past famines, we want that comforting feeling of having many things to help us, and so we collect bits and pieces and we don't let go of them.

Hoarding may even be a form of replacing people. I read in a paper that, if we need to, we substitute 'inanimate things that can never run away for intimate others that might'.

I don't hoard, I don't buy so much. Still, my computer is filled with digital carts in this season.

I wasn't shopping in summer. Back then my hands were filled with flowers, but now they're not. Now my hands are cold and empty when I'm outside. They're cold when I'm inside too. These cold hands are getting stiff, they're telling me of an age when I won't be able to fumble with my buttons, when my mother will be dead and my father will be dead and the dog will be dead and who knows about him and maybe that scares me. Maybe that's why I want to sit stroking bits of cloth.

Certainly I am feeling empty. Certainly I can't find my ancestors while inside typing at these computer keys. Computer keys are a bit like piano keys. They're like piano keys and nothing more. And how many along my line had such an instrument? Only one or two of my most recent relatives have ever played.

Maybe I should have bought a piano instead of bones, when I went online. Opening the glossy lid, in the right light those piano keys would shine like the nacreous insides of mussel shells. A piano is so expensive though.

But the Roman ring that came in the post two weeks ago—its signet needs only the gentlest pressing for the mind to go reeling above perfumed pools and into the original backstreet where I imagine its bronze shape was so roughly chiselled. On fondling this ring while stottering along the hedged streets, a blacksmith's hands are chipping four lines *there*, into a paw. Rolling such an item round the melamine surface of the kitchen table, the workshop comes back again and again. This Roman ring. I love it. I love it. The imagination animates it.

It's confusing that a feeling of immanence can come from material goods.

I think I'm meant to hate the material. I'm meant to know what Blake knew. That the imagination is 'the real & eternal World of which this Vegetable Universe is but a faint shadow'. Yet I cannot say with certainty that having a moon-shaped necklace would *not* produce transcendent feelings. And if a moon was flashing there on my chest, it might catch a passer-by's eye. Dark jumpers and celestial necklaces. If I was wearing an outfit like that, what might someone walking past me see? Sheep tumbling about the night fields.

Blaeberry

November 26

This cookbook by René Redzepi is stylish. On its fabric cover there's a black-and-white illustrated hand that appears to be caressing a tender bush. Inside are recipes for fermented waxworms and black apples. The directions are quite complicated, and I don't trust that I'd have the patience to make them. Instead I've taken the easiest recipe from the book.

A few evenings ago, by the light of a candle, I tipped all the frozen berries from summer and some salt in a jar. I sloshed the ingredients about a bit. I touched those star dimples one last time. I thought about the flowers they once were. Then I looked at the ice dissolving against my hands. And though I knew I was meant to weigh the berries down with a Ziploc bag filled with water, I did not do that. I did not want to be reminded of goldfish and funfairs and striped socks and falling yellow ducks. And so I left the berries in contact with the air.

The jar of berries and salt on the shelf has been glowing quietly ever since.

A thread of white fur has been forming around each minuscule star. Now the berries look like newborn seals capering in the surf. That wasn't meant to happen. Still, I know it's better to scupper plans from the off. Scupper everything and let furred malevolences grow. Then there can be no sense of disappointment when the inevitable happens. Do things only a little well and no one will ever know how you once wished for life to be.

November 29

The purple juice was salvageable. I squeezed the furry lot through muslin into a bowl. There was so much liquid I was able to boil some of it on the stovetop with vinegar and store it in a jar. I brushed some across five large pieces of watercolour paper which I then left to dry in the hallway. I took the papers onto the hill this afternoon. I silently watched a line of female deer being nudged through the snow by an antlered male. Then I brought out a basket filled with various pebbles and sticks and placed those objects on paper—the grey-blue wash was soon turning pale beneath the weak sun. The weak light was touching the backs of my legs too.

The pebbles and sticks obscured the sunlight in places. The paper there remained dark blue. The colour there is really vibrating. There's really no end to transformation.

Cabbage

December 1

Take two frilled purple cabbage heads from the basket, chop them up and weigh out the salt. Fist ingredients in a bowl till they're juicing. Scoop the mixture into a just-boiled jar. Weigh the cruciferous ribbons down properly this time and send them right to the back of the cupboard.

Let the stars go careening six times round. Cabbage strips will come out soft and glistening. They'll be sauerkraut kimchi kyslá kapusta kapusta kiszona. This transformation has little to do with you, and everything to do with bacteria. And still you feel you could lasso a wolf.

Utilising this recipe that goes back perhaps to the ancient Tatars, I don't feel I'm living in the past by re-enacting their methods. Sharpening a knife in the darkness. Watching things glisten. There's a future where preserving cabbage may be necessary, and I'd like to pretend I can prepare.

December 6

I've pickled everything in the cupboards there is to pickle—the carrots the garlic the chanterelles the radishes. Now there's no vessel left to fill.

December 7

Strained oats and water through a cloth bag. Milk came gushing cold through my fingers.

Next time I'll warm it to porridge. I'll pretend a lip of cream is rising in the bucket.

Stew

December 9

This week, by the light of one candle, I made a stew. Unable to see if anything was burning at the bottom of the pot, for an hour I stood and stirred the vegetables on the gentlest heat possible. Then I brought two bowls over to the table.

We ate in near darkness. With our eyes quiet, I thought we might better notice that potatoes possess the same aromatic notes found in persimmon, black truffles, and rye.

I asked him if he could taste rye.

He shook his head.

I was not more sensitive to such aromas either.

I liked being in the darkness though. The darkness felt relaxing. Now it was winter I could lie about in my dress and stockings and that was much better. Yes I liked the darkness. Not too long ago, it was quite normal to be in the darkness all winter. It was normal for all the street lights to stay off when there was a full moon. It was like that in Stromness when my great-grandfather was the postman. He went out handing penny letters in the evenings, a small glass lantern attached to his lapel so he could read the addresses. On full moon nights, Ali Thomson the lamplighter got the evening off. He left his oilskins by the door. And the townspeople went out still. Between shadows and silver puddles, they wandered along the bright harbour.

There are municipalities still providing such experiences. There is at least one. In the mountain city of Saadat Shahr in Iran, street lights are turned off on clear nights so citizens can participate in stargazing parties.

I should write to the mayor to see if we can keep the lights off here sometimes. I won't mind if he laughs at my request. He does not know who I am. I might suggest the town grocery stores stock torches for striding home with. Bending flames into night's ears, I'd feel as strong as an ancient one. I'd plunge death into soldiers' chests. And I'd rather see stars than street lights. I'd rather know the dark, blind comforts of the earth than anything. I'd be imagining night folding itself over forests and rivers and longhouses and a girl sitting by the fire. She's turning a gold foil figurine this way and that until her favourite guldgubber is stalking her fingers.

A little girl ten centuries later is doing the same with figurines she's pinched from chocolate wrappers. In the candlelight she feels them dancing. The candle beneath the carousel is burning. The heat is rising and four brass angels are ringing. I can stick my fingers in the flames while Mum is turned towards the cooking pot. I can go so low and slow when nobody's watching.

The scientists know we want the darkness. They do. Whenever they are trying to make the rats sad, they put them on an elevated pedestal, up to the light. Rats don't like the light. And nor do we. We want to be running low to the ground, down in the flickering shadows.

All through winter, I like it very dark. Just one candle and a scoop of apple basking on the table. Glossy plums and gingerbread heaped in pewter bowls. A dish of salt. One walnut.

Blake

December 15

This Sunday he woke early so we could read William Blake together. It's good to drink a lot of Turkish coffee while reading such things. Then you're really oscillating while flicking the pages. These pages have been bringing me into the tail end of the eighteenth century, where a man at a desk is scratching words backwards on sheets of copper. He's watching the candle on his desk—its flames are towering like irises. They're sending him into the palm of his hand. Now he's surrounding curled letters with images of women and fires. He's etching the sun till it's sending men spinning. He's creating birds, buttocks, black rivers.

In Blake's surviving self-portrait, he looks like a preternaturally intense baby. Strange boy, seeing angels in the tree boughs as a child. Strange son of a shopkeeper; he was thirty-three years old when he made this book that's in our hands now. He and his wife Catherine initially made just nine copies of *The Marriage of Heaven and Hell*, each one by hand. Now I suppose there are many thousands of printed versions floating about the world's shelves.

Our copy has a black and shining cover and a yellow line for a border. My eyes are feeling huge just looking at it.

Samuel Taylor Coleridge made a key to his reactions while reading one of Blake's books.

I signified 'It gave me great pleasure'.
H, 'still greater'.

Ĥ, 'and greater still'.
Θ, 'in the highest degree'.

One poem within the collection was rated 'Θ: yea Θ + Θ!'

Θ: yea Θ + Θ! to all of Blake's words. To night visions boiling over with flames and colour and muscled swirling serpents. To starburst words intensifying every feeling.

Blake, I cannot imagine you properly. The puzzles of your thoughts are somewhat mysterious to me, but I don't mind burrowing near them. What are you saying? Something about energy being the thing? Something about the divine reaching towards us through the imagination? The divine reaching us all through the imagination, that's it.

Blake, I want to talk to you, you who lived before the gas lamps, you with your words that went sloping into the rhythmic dark. I could feel you with us yesterday. As my husband and I went walking in the deep cold, there was a rare hushed energy about us both. Listening to the wind as we drifted through the woods, I knew we were immersed in your world still.

There'd been no one on the snowy path for hours. And then that man came along. Asking if we had a light. Asking if we knew it was getting dark.

Something about his jacket. Something about his hat. I fidgeted with my gloves, my heart pounding. Then as soon as he was out of earshot, I exploded. I said men were always taking on the role of expert out here. They were always saying *the summit is not far now*. They were saying *you're almost there*. These men. They don't know where I'm going or what I'm planning. They don't know I might be winding my way round to the river so I can have a lie down. Sometimes I am.

My husband couldn't understand my point. Of course the man was concerned about our abilities to withstand time outdoors—my backpack was made of wicker and he appeared to be dressed as a Moomin character.

Checking we had lights. I just didn't believe that was what it was about. That man. He just needed an audience for his desired role of expert to come to fruition. Yet I did not feel like being a silhouette to his projection, and he should not have forced me to assume that position.

Anyway, I said, I had brought a light.

My husband was quite impressed that I had brought a light. It wasn't the sort of thing I did. Normally I left practical things to him.

I rummaged in my backpack and brought it out.

'You brought your candle lantern,' he said.

'It's a light, isn't it?'

'I thought you meant a headlamp.'

'Headlamps aren't beautiful,' I replied, opening the lantern's small glass door.

I suppose I must have been tilting the lantern at an angle, for the tealight I'd stored inside immediately tipped into the soft snow.

I knew even as I sifted that the candle would not appear again before springtime.

I felt quite scared then, for the trees were weaving into a silken mass with the rapidly darkening air. There was just us, drifting through the deep snow. In the dark. In the cold. In the dark and the cold with no torch and hardly any food and no blankets and I was panicking saying *are we safe*—I kept saying *are we*—

He just whispered *snow glows*. I looked at the darkening path. At snow the green of a male eider's nape. At snow glowing on every tree bough, and the wavering outlines of the trees nuzzling one another in the falling darkness, and the big moon rising, sending shadows from every pine, and the little hunched tree in front of me turning into a babushka holding her snowy arms open in invitation. Rummaging through my backpack for Blake's book, I held it up against her in the dark, whispering, 'The imagination is the divine place where I meet you.'

Solstice

December 21

It had been a long day of kittens. I was feeling a bit murky even before I'd walked up the hill. Even before I'd reached the spot where Maria had set up her witch party, I was feeling a bit dredged up. It was a nice night, though. With the papery moon and the stars flashing. With Maria and Inga and Laura and Elena sitting around the fir tree with candles set out in front of them. Inga had brought a black cake in a biscuit tin. She said in the past times the people would set an actual log alight to symbolise the sun on the winter solstice. At some point, quite recently perhaps, a yule log had become dessert. She'd heard about it on the radio.

We each ate two slices of cake, and then we did not know what to do.

We sat about on blankets for a bit, then Maria took her phone from her coat pocket. She slid her index finger across the screen until she'd found the song she was looking for.

The sounds of a woman throat-singing began to weave through the air.

Get up! Maria was saying, clapping her hands.
I didn't want to get up.
Get up! she said, squeezing my shoulder.
I got up.

Maria was kicking her legs in an awkward jig while shouting *Come on! Come on!* to the woman's singing being distorted through the speakers. I watched our shadows carouselling alongside us.

When Inga and I walked down the hill later, I said I couldn't understand how Maria could have done that. Making us dance like that, what was all that about?

Inga kicked some snow at me and said I had not had to dance.

I said Maria could go and get eaten by a crow for all I cared. I'd never liked her. And the revival of throat singing was so young no? It's not at all long since Christian missionaries tried to break Inuit cultures. When they saw girls clasping one another's arms, bouncing lightly and singing, they declared the girls' actions satanic. They suppressed the threads of an ancient practice. 'As the caterpillar chooses the fairest leaves to lay her eggs on, so the priest lays his curse on the fairest joys.' That's what Blake said. That's often what happens.

Ancient arts belonging to others just don't go with those speakers, don't go with our dancing. Sticking needles in that boundless cloth like that. It's not on. If you go plunging your needle in, thinking a stitch is just a stitch and it doesn't matter what you do, then it's very obvious you'll cause havoc in no time.

I can't stand that we cavorted insincerely through the thinnest part of the year like that. As for all those white-robed misters at Stonehenge who are out tonight, what's that about? Some historian in Bavaria goes for a walk in the Renaissance and comes across a grove? Finds stones engraved with images of cloaked men and imagines he's discovered the prayer site of ancient druids. Has his findings disseminated as truth for years and years, has them disseminated far and wide until it doesn't matter that he more likely came across the ruins of the Speinshart monastery and its carvings of various Franconian prophets.

There are some who'd admit they just like the feel of the cloth. They just like toying with it. They'd admit we can't know very much about the druids at all. Well alright. That's alright, but the new ways that attempt an emulation of the old and call it truth are distortions. And I don't think we should be getting our needles in any faint holes. I don't think we should pretend to know what we very well can't. Those new books that pretend to be historically accurate. What's that about? Just say it's a lark. Tell the journalist at Stonehenge you're dressed in a cloak because you're a clown. Admit you're a destroyer of the past and your white robes are mangling whatever threads might still be dangling.

So many patterns of life we've been smothering. So many messes we've left for others to go untangling. Our jig on a hill was making a mockery of throat singing despite that not being the intention. We shouldn't have done that. Inga said she didn't know what I was going on about. She said I had to get a grip. I looked down at my boots then and knew I was jealous. I was jealous of anyone who felt they knew what they were supposed to be doing tonight. Other cultures seem to have stronger traditions for this time of year. And I am envious of any man in a Novosibirsk graveyard who's keeping his corpse-father warm by building a fire. Maybe he hears talking.

An Iranian boy is reciting poetry with his family while the moon rises white beyond the curtains. A woman in Kyoto is running a bath. Already she has put new sheets on the bed and looked out her best pyjamas, the ones with blue piping.

I'm jealous of them all. I'm jealous of everyone at Stonehenge. Photographers from *The Sun* and *The Star* and *The Mirror* take photos so readers the next day can laugh at them over breakfast. Yet how beautiful it must be to chant with others outside. It must be a really special evening. More special than laughing.

I'm beginning to feel more and more impressed by Maria, who did, after all, go to the effort of bringing us all together tonight. She danced in the darkness without embarrassment. I'm impressed by anyone who can do that. And I think I do understand why she chose to play Inuit music instead of honouring solstice traditions from her own ancestors. A spotlight has been placed on the priests, lawmakers and landowners who terrorised Indigenous people from here to Bolivia to Samoa. That spotlight is long overdue. And settlers with European roots now tend to feel guilty about their ancestral history.

It's become common to state here that Judeo-Christian culture is responsible for the modern world's ills. There's so much truth to that. Still, that telling does not include the minor European stories that were long running beneath the paradigm—or the incantations of every peasant who was carrying on the old, pre-Reformation ways right into the nineteenth century. They were secretly praising every living creature as soon as they were waking up in the mornings. Their worldview was violently suppressed by John Knox in 1560. But people were still secretly bowing to the sun and the moon after that. After the Reformation, the Hebridean ones who doffed their caps to the sun were being much mocked by children. If they openly viewed the moon as the 'glorious lamp of the poor', they were being viewed as numpties by the young. One old man in Arisaig was jeered at for bowing to the moon and sun. But did he stop? He did not.

'When the sun would rise on the tops of the peaks he would put off his head-covering and he would bow down his head, giving glory for the goodness of the light to the children and animals of the world.'

When the old ways were crushed, when the chants were silenced and had to be crooned beneath the breath, they didn't vanish.

Though for centuries, non-dominant beliefs were furiously condemned, there were still people intoning the old words in low and tremulous cadences. To pray, they generally went to a secluded place; into a closet, into an outhouse, or into the lee of a knoll or a bay.

Alexander Carmichael knew men and women of eighty or ninety walking one or two miles to the seashore each day to join their voices with the ocean's song. They went to praise the waves. They secretly thanked every nut and flower.

Alexander Carmichael wrote of a woman from Harris:

'Mary Macrae was rather under than over middle height, but strongly and symmetrically formed. She often walked with companions, after the work of the day was done, distances of ten and fifteen miles to a dance, and after dancing all night walked back again to the work of the morning fresh and vigorous as if nothing unusual had occurred. She was a faithful servant and an admirable worker, and danced at her leisure and carolled at her work like "Fosgag Mhoire", Our Lady's lark, above her.

'The people of Harris had been greatly given to old lore and to the old ways of their fathers, reciting and singing, dancing and merry-making; but a reaction occurred, and Mary Macrae's old-world ways were abjured and condemned.

'The bigots of an iron age called her simple art a crime.

'But Mary Macrae heeded not, and went on in her own way, singing her songs and ballads, intoning her hymns and incantations, and chanting her own "port-a-bial", mouth music, and dancing to her own shadow when nothing better was available.'

He wrote, *'I love to think of this brave, kind woman, with her strong Highland characteristics and her proud Highland spirit. She was a true type of a grand person.'*

Dancing to her own shadow when nothing better was available. How I love this image. How I love to feel these stitches left by Mary Macrae from Harris. Stitches of all the people dancing to their own shadows—I'd like to pull their stories into the light. I'd like to live in the shadows with them.

On leaving the woods and entering town, Inga said she was planning to get her bath so hot she might faint. I said that was a great idea. I wanted to get a bit dizzy too.

When I got in I took off my long johns, my velvet dress, my boots and my socks. I made a liquorice tea. I ran the bath. In the water I soon was euphoric. For having positioned the candle just so on the bath tray, the shadows of the taps were now being flung against the tiled walls like Baby Dinosaur in his high chair.

Why was I thinking about Baby Dinosaur?

I wanted to think about the old prayers.

I wanted to think about a woman in Kyoto who was also having a bath.

After work, Minae spent a tiny fortune at Momento Mori. She purchased bath salts and beeswax candles, then at the market on the way home, she bought seven yuzu fruits. She tried not to look at the receipts. The price of everything was going up and up. A thousand yen a pound just for the fruits! She supposed they must symbolise the sun, being so gold and fresh. Still, the cost of it all made her feel a bit ill. She'd been feeling off since the ride into work, when a beautiful man with plum lips looked right past her. Her heart had hardened against him then, against everyone.

It was much better to be alone, she decided. When there were no people around, she wished no malice on a single soul.

The night before, while Nanae packed her rucksack for her weekend with Akio, Minae had put on her old grey dress and cleaned. Moving clockwise, she swept insects into the dustpan in the kitchen. She sprayed vinegar and baking soda over the tiles. She got rid of a jacket with moss growing in its pocket. When she was done, the grouting still looked grimy and there were still dead flies inside the bathroom light fixture.

Nanae listened to Minae's laments. She looked thoughtful for a bit, then came back with the salt crystal lamp from her room. She plugged it into the razor socket in the bathroom and said, *That's better.* It really was. In the soft, dim light, you could hardly see the mould. The whole room gleamed gold.

Now Nanae was on the train to Itō with Akio, and Minae's best pyjamas lay folded on the bed, and she had tea and seven yuzu fruits cut into fourteen on the bath tray, and the bathwater was running, and the whole apartment was hers alone.

It felt good to be alone. What had she done on her last weekend like this? In the morning she'd cut up the back of a cereal box into sixteen pieces. On the plain side of each card she'd drawn a fox. She'd drawn foxes from quite big to small. On the last cards she'd just been pressing the pencil nib and making orange dots. Then she began writing a story to go with each card.

'Foxes will bring you good fortune, but only if you catch their tail.'

'There is a country, far away, where people watch dawn mist rise from the rivers. When they see this, they say to each other, "*The foxes are up and making coffee*."'

'The aurora is made up of foxtails sweeping arcs into the sky.'

After making her cards, Minae had gone for a walk by the river. She followed the water till the leaves were stars and the frogs were burping. On an overgrown path leading up the hill, posters began to appear on the trees. They said,

LOOK INSIDE YOUR HEART.

WHAT WILL YOU FIND.

MAYBE SOMETHING WONDERFUL.

(only you can know.)

The posters made Minae feel like maybe there was really something wonderful inside her. Like maybe she did know.

She followed winding steps to a temple. A woman in a threadbare dress was holding on to a cabbage. She put it down when she saw she had a visitor. She encouraged Minae to ring the bell. Apparently its vibrations could be heard through the valley, and others would feel at peace on hearing it. Minae shook her head. She didn't want to ring the bell. She went to sit on the veranda.

Minae took out her last card and wrote, 'I will always remember the warm feeling of your floor, and how you let me touch your big feet with my small ones'. Then one by one she lit the cards with matches so her grandmother might read them.

A wax wall like the outer moat of a castle had begun to appear around the top of the lit candle on Minae's bath tray. The candle's warm light was filtering through the wooden lattice. Now light was flowing along Minae's thighs and up her stomach. In that wet little room, she was in the bottom of a cave. She was in a cave in a deep, dark forest. The tip of the flame was flickering like a fox's tail. It was a fox's tail very bright and pulsing through the woods towards the sea. Its bright light was casting along her legs, it was throbbing and lighting up her pubic hair like frogspawn. She was amid foxes and frogs, yes, and in the steaming sea Minae was a fish. A fish in a tide pool. A fish curved and firm and sheening amid plants swaying and yellow crabs and seaweed. And the silvery taps were starfish. Starfish raising the tips of their legs. Their lilac legs curling up. O the starfish were curling. They were breathing through every body-channel. O they were breathing O.

Minae pushed her feet ecstatically against the bath rim as she watched a spider abseiling onto the teapot. It creeped across the tray and onto the bathroom tiles. Its plump body was the size of a currant, its shadow the size of a plum. It was folding its legs and its shadow was morphing into a bird of paradise, a pelican, a flapper girl. This spider was turning into a woman folding and unfolding her legs in a deckchair. Was its heart bursting as its shadow suddenly transformed into a moʻai overlooking Easter Island?

Minae decided its heart was indeed bursting. A new feeling was bursting through her as three words spun outwards.

'Shadows are love,' Minae said, pirouetting her index fingers upon the foam.

Minae tried and failed to make the words withstand the sweeping lights of logic. She closed her eyes and slid further into the warm water until her mouth was near its surface. 'Shadows follow me wherever I go,' she whispered finally, revving the bathwater.

Yule

December 25

Mum and Dad just emailed about deer moving past their morning window. They know I like to hear of them.

Now they're getting ready for the big day. They've cleaned out the shelves of the icehouse. They've polished the knives and arranged the candlesticks, the holly, and the salad leaves. Later on the pudding will be set aflame.

If I was there, there'd be twenty-six hands clapping. I'd be arranging the salad leaves and carrying the plates.

Now all these people I love exist only in the place where dreams are made. And I am but a dream to them. And I won't be helping Isla put on her party crown today. I won't be watching snow float onto the sea tomorrow. I won't be opening cloudberry liqueurs or carving persimmons or finding snails for my nephews and nieces to follow. There won't be any of that. It won't be minus two outside with the beds cool and the stars chattering nonsense to a silent house. It won't be all lovely and cold with the only heat coming from fires and cast iron radiators that need bleeding with special keys. I won't spend winter under many blankets, huddled in cold rooms. It's twenty-seven degrees in his mother's house, and the trees in the yards are grey and bristling, and outside it's minus forty and I don't think it's possible to experience a temperature change of nearly seventy degrees from inside to out without feeling crazed.

The puppy vomited behind a plant pot yesterday. I felt like joining her.

I wish I had kitten work to do.
That'd take my mind off things.

If I was back in our flat I'd hide in the bath.

I can't have a bath here, I can't use up all the hot water as a guest. If I did they'd be imagining me with my chin tilted on the acrylic rim and they'd be asking him *is she alright is she though?*

Heating vents bordering the perimeter of the bedroom carpet, I've never seen such a thing. It's too efficient. It's too dry and my cold cream is sticking to my tights. Static is shooting me every time I open a door and the only thing for it is to sit on his childhood bed with the puppy, throwing orange peels down the vents for the monkeys. I've been placing things on the vents too. Glass bowls filled with water and cedar oil. Damp rags.

I know a good daughter-in-law would be downstairs helping get things ready for dinner. He is a good son. He's been ferrying his sisters all over the place; he's been hoovering and chopping up all sorts. I know I shouldn't be upstairs hiding while feigning sickness. But I've never had much interest in charming anyone.

Actually when we first got here I floated about the kitchen going, *Can I do anything what can I do?* I did a few little tasks until it became very clear it would be better for everyone if I just brought forth a little cough and went upstairs—for in no time I'd put the crystal in the wrong place and scratched the good cutlery.

He's been quietly bringing me oranges ever since, though he knows as well as I do that I'm not sick in that way.

Something about the aroma of those peels and the intense heat in this room has been bringing me back into Greece. Into wearing black dresses, into pulling off greasy tablecloths and clearing up beer bottles. Into sleeping in that caravan at night, the one the local teenagers got stoned in and the taverna cooks changed in.

I don't remember the name of the waiter who crept in. When he entered my sleeping quarters it was late and he was wearing only his boxer shorts. He was smoking. It was the smell of his cigarette that woke me. I asked him to go and he left. I've experienced worse. And I could see why he'd got mixed messages. I was always asking him about his country's women, about the hill towns and the Roman ruins. I could see how he might have got the wrong idea. Whoever could care that much about Albania?

I just didn't expect to be thinking of him while stuck on the edge of this icy city. The memories seeping into me with this heat.

Well there will always be little surprises in life. I just didn't imagine a desire to travel would render me motionless in some man's childhood bedroom within the decade. Though I suppose it's a common story. It happened to Isabelle Eberhardt even. In her early twenties, she crossed the Mediterranean on an adventure of her own making. It was July 1900. Alone on the ferry from Marseille to Algiers, she stretched out on an empty deck, looked out at her surroundings, and wrote, 'I feel alone, free, and detached from everything in the world, and I'm happy.' Her Algeria trip was intended to be a voyage of study and curiosity. She planned to smoke *kief* and eventually set up a solitary owl's nest somewhere, far away from people. There she would isolate her soul 'for months and months from all human contact' because to her, 'to be alone is to be free'.

Of course, when she did find herself alone, in rented rooms, it was often not solitude she found. She was often writing of a sadness that was boundless, of an abandonment she felt in the middle of the vast universe. She wrote,

'What pains me most is the prodigious changeability of my nature and the really distressing instability of my states of mind, which follow one another with alarming speed.'

Because she was afraid of herself, she was always dusting herself off in search of new adventures. She'd be burning across the Sahara like black glitter, on trains, on horseback, on whatever money she had. She'd be buying skinned hares from Bedouins, or couch-surfing with sheikhs, or throwing the last of her cash from town windows.

Born in 1877 in a large and gloomy house on Geneva's edge, her biological father was not the Russian general her mother had married but, secretly, the household tutor. Alexandre Trophimowsky was a controlling ex-priest who isolated the family from the outside world and insisted on cropped hair and trousers for Isabelle—the only girl. She was given a rigorous education, including lessons in six languages. She learned about religion and anarchy, metaphysics and philosophy. Trophimowsky read the Koran with her from a young age.

There was not much obvious love to go around in that house beneath the Jura Mountains. In the lonely nights of her teenage years, Isabelle escaped her physical circumstances by writing stories.

For Isabelle, travelling across the Algerian desert was freedom. She loved those short, moonlit nights spent sleeping at Moorish cafés with 'nothing but infinite sky for a roof and warm ground for a bed'. She loved the desert—that sad and grey, wind-shaped place. The 'sickly light pale as a convalescent's smile', the eagles that 'hung like golden nails affixed to the incandescent sky'.

While travelling, Isabelle wrote loosely veiled fiction about young people who had the terrible freedom of moving through the world with no ties. In one story, a wayfarer walked until there were 'no prayers, no medicines, merely the ineffable happiness of dying'. In another, a man escaped his cruel father by joining the Foreign Legion. Isabelle's characters were like her, tough and lonely. And they were always male—so the stories would be believable.

The thrill of sensation—for Isabelle it came from dressing as a man in a white burnous and tasting cigarettes and anisette and other bodies. It lay in the intoxication of running from the French police in anti-colonial protests turned violent. Playing piano in garrison bars. Scratching goats while listening to local women tell stories in their hillside homes.

She loved hook-ups; there were many of them. But with Slimène Ehnni it was different. An Algerian cavalryman her age, Slimène was gentle. Slimène was kind. From August 1900 they were meeting in secret at night. In the gardens outside the town of El Oued, they'd have sex. Afterwards, their heads resting on pillows of sand, they'd talk about their dreams for the future. His arms would curve around her back and she'd watch, astonished, as a new feeling began to rise through her chest. What a feeling, the beginnings of love.

Isabelle and Slimène got married so she could stay in Algeria.

She lived with her mother-in-law for a bit; she lived with Slimène's sisters. Don't know where he was. Away training in some garrison I suppose. As I remember it, his mother and sisters were cruel to Isabelle and they were always fighting with her, but what could she do? She stayed for as long as she could bear it.

My husband, when he last came up the stairs to see me, said, on being pressed, that he liked Isabelle's bravado. He liked her writing and her love of animals. 'And didn't the French try to get her assassinated by sabre?'

When he went back downstairs, I started cutting up the black card I'd brought with me to his mother's house. With a white pencil, I drew a tarot-sized version of Isabelle as best I could. I painted a halo round her head. I wrote her first name with an Orthodox ε. I painted her stubborn, snubby face and wrote the word 'Vengeance' on her cap.

I thought of Isabelle leaving her mother-in-law's and moving to Marseille, dressing in boy's clothes and working as a docker—the other workers half-naked by the violet water. They drank wine and ate market food cooked on top of collapsed petrol cans. The freedom to be part of that scene was, she wrote, the only happiness accessible to her nature.

Why'd I come here? Because he had a voice like a nightingale? When he sang that night in the jungle, he turned the crowds invisible. I found him later in the alley. My heart was pounding as I went up to him. Ever since he's been pulling shapes from the stars for me. He's been spotting every wolf in the grass. Yet he can never be enough. He cannot be my father. He cannot be my mother.

This week I did not sit down for tea beside my father and I did not hold my mother's hand.

When we met his eyes were black. His teeth were snow white and I was too young to think of loved ones getting older, of nieces and nephews being born in the coming years.

Now Isla is getting so big and Dad is sick and I've killed our relationship that exists beneath language's surface—that thing that lies privately between us, that cannot be felt through words.

This keyboard I spend my days touching has given me an unreal relationship with my family. By allowing us to communicate so easily, it has made the unbearable nature of being apart just bearable enough.

In the electronics district of Tokyo, I've heard Shinto priests in lacquered headgear will provide a cleansing ceremony for any device. I don't think my computer should get blessed. Why should I honour it? Oh I know I'm a miserable wretch. What's pressing on me now? My Seville marmalade, my miraculous bread? I have a whole box of beeswax beneath the flat sofa, and bright and most suckable candles. It's true there've been no portraits passed down in my family; no sapphires or tassels or cloaks of glistening Lyon silk, yet look at me now.

It's just that I suppose I'd like to just go off for years and return and go and return. Alexandra David-Néel did so when she was married. She worked as an opera singer in Asia through her twenties. She became a Buddhist then married a French railroad engineer named Philippe Néel in Tunis in 1904. Now she had everything her childhood in Paris had taught her to want—love, money, a palm-filled villa in North Africa, days filled with luncheons and couturier appointments.

But she was unravelling with headaches, nausea, exhaustion. For what she actually wanted was contemplation and adventure. In an attempt to satiate her desires, she'd go off and meditate in 'perfect detachment' for an hour each day. She wanted more of that. While her husband was away healing in Vichy's thermal baths on holiday, she left for Asia to further her Buddhist education. She studied with the Gomchen of Lachen, a hermit sorcerer who, it was said, could fly through the air and kill a person with a glance. She meditated in a mountain cave for many winters. With a young Nepali monk, she disguised herself as a Tibetan peasant and set off to the forbidden city of Lhasa. They crested snowy passes. They shouted '*Gé-o!*' ('May all beings be happy!') into the frozen sky. She was not forgetting her dear Philippe when she said this. And she was always sending him letters about her travels. Also would it be okay if he sent her a little more money?

Here my husband comes now, up the stairs, with tea for me. I won't dare wound him with a single word of discontent. My unhappiness is not because of anything he's done. He barely latched his finger round my balloon when he tugged and pulled.

Drifting around—staying at this beach hostel or that—the sky was warm and blue for a long time. And yet I could feel with the passing years that I was floating very far from earth, and that the air was getting thin.

Now every night I can sleep beside my husband, and though he is not my mother or a big golden spider, I love him.

I do think meeting him will always be the great happiness and great sadness of my life.

I do think there are a few angry women inside me.

As children they were the ones dreaming up fantasies in dark nooks. They were wayward. Then they were mothers.

They're awake in me. All those ancestors who might have very much liked the chance to go gallivanting. They don't just wake up when I'm gathering berries with Inga in summer. There are ones who know when an opportunity's been squandered. Because for how long in all of human history have women genuinely had the chance to drift about for no reason? Even a century ago, good luck trying that without great wealth or a religious proviso.

'Ever since I was five years old,' David-Néel wrote in her memoir, 'I wished to move out of the narrow limits in which, like all children of my age, I was then kept. I craved to go beyond the garden gate, to follow the road that passed it by, and to set out for the Unknown.'

Of course, she was able to do so because she was brave and rich and she lived not too long ago.

I'm really the first, I think, to be born in a time when you don't have to be daring to go off somewhere new.

Now I'm in a strange house with a man. All those ancestors with their hands in mine, with their mouths and their tears. They're in my heart I know.

Though surely some must be wondering how my life involves so little physical labour. How to tell them the work of making clothes and gathering food is outsourced to women in distant countries? That's why I have been able to do what my ancestors could not.

Invisible mothers in oppressed nations are caring for me. They're sewing my clothes, my rucksacks, my boots.

They've been picking fruits and nuts for me, they've been gathering and drying my tea leaves.

The facts of their lives destroy the illusion of my little pleasures being wholesome.

And I think I've got Alexandra David-Néel's story all wrong. Though I make fun of the cavalier way she seemed to treat her husband, I don't think she'd like that we stake stories like hers onto narratives about how free a woman can be. The yak butter and rock shelters and people who sheltered her were absolutely intertwined with her. She knew that. She knew there could be no individual freedom if everyone was not free. And so she knew she was not free.

I have not said sorry and thank you nearly enough in my life. Now I'm looking at a children's lifetime of things on his bedroom shelves, I'm saying sorry and thank you—to all the people who made them, to the trees that made these books, and to the instruments, sorry sorry and thank you.

I will need to say the same to him when he next comes up the stairs—for he is like a mother to me, doing so much for me.

Sock

January 2

This week I learned how to darn socks. I darned all my socks, and then I darned his socks.

Skate

January 9

Yesterday we woke at dawn and drove back to the mountains. On the way, we camped by a frozen lake. There were small gold birds in the pine trees, and the clouds were turning golden too as we set up the tent and settled inside it. I rubbed my feet together in my sleeping bag to stay warm. The feeling each time I momentarily managed to find relief from the cold was a kind of rhapsody, and my mind was soon drifting pleasantly towards thoughts of a diary I'd been reading over Christmas. *A Woman in the Polar Night* was written by a woman from Vienna named Christiane Ritter. She sailed off to Svalbard in the 1930s to join her husband. He'd initially travelled to the Arctic as a scientist. He'd decided to stay on as a hunter in the wilderness. When the boat dropped her off on the island, she was distraught. Her new home was not at all cosy and charming. It was a decrepit black-roofed cabin she was to share with her husband and his gruff Norwegian pal Karl.

The stove barely warmed them. The windowpanes were constantly frosted to whiteness. The seal meat they were to eat for their tea each night tasted like fish mixed with dog. Ritter felt seized with an unutterable terror at the situation she had got herself into. She was so sure they'd all become vitamin-deficient. She was so sure she wouldn't be able to stand it. When the men went off hunting in the winter darkness, she was on her own. And what did she get up to? There were little tasks for her to do. For example she collected glacier ice and thawed it into drinking water. Sometimes she darned old socks and gloves. Every day she marked the course of the night on scraps of paper—67 days without sun, 92 days without sun, 119 days without sun, 134 days without sun. It was not like she had books to read or visitors to expect or furniture to clean. Mostly she just lay wrapped in fur in her bunk and listened to the silence. There in the 'holy quiet'—that was how she described it—with the full moon rising, she would feel herself dissolving in moonlight; she would feel herself being eaten up by the moon; her entire consciousness was being penetrated by the brightness, she was being drawn into the moon itself. That was how it felt. There in the darkness, in the silence of the polar world, her heart and mind were turning towards a permanent state of elevation. And she found she didn't want to go back to Vienna. She didn't want to go back to her old life at all. She pitied the women of Europe, including her past self, 'who besides being worn out by the unending struggle against soot and dust, moths and mice, also feel themselves obliged to keep up appearances'.

When we got in late the next morning, I took a shower, drank some tea, put my things away, then went straight out to meet Inga at the pond outside town. She was bending one leg and gliding on the other. Her red dress was twisting like a feather as I skated out to meet her. We moved beneath the copper trees, chatting and looking for beavers swimming beneath the ice. Tremors were shooting up my legs and into my chest in the calm cold air.

I loved being near her. She said every night of the holidays, she'd watched the sunset over the beach with her grandmother.

Suddenly I heard what she was saying. I felt my socks sliding down inside my boots, the ice growing very dark.

'You will be by the ocean all the time then,' I said.

Tangerine

January 23

This week I fashioned a lamp from a tangerine and a tablespoon of olive oil. The white pith running up the centre of the fruit acted as a natural wick, but a seam had split down the side. Now there's olive oil on my tights.

I suppose this will be my life then. Trying to fend off the dog as she jumps up and tries to lick me. Going about with olive oil on my tights.

Book

February 1

Today I took a book outside. The hair on my head fell onto its pages as shadows. The penumbral tips of my strands grazed the words—

Market
Furlough
Kiss

I don't know what it meant. It meant nothing.

Note

February 10

This week I left a notebook and pen in a bag on top of the hill. Perhaps I'll make a new friend that way.

But I don't want a new friend.

Chop

February 13

Today I chopped up our chopping board into very tiny pieces.
Now we have no chopping board.
Now he's angry with me.

Lune

February 15

This week I followed the moon as it grew smaller.
I'll do this with my whole life then.
This will be my whole life.
Following the moon in the deep cold.
Growing smaller.
Seeing only myself,
My discoloured lips,
Not thinking about Napoleon's frozen army in the same deep cold,
as they plunged into Russian winter in thin embroidered coats
And ate their own horses mixed with gunpowder for the salt

I'll not imagine their misery
Their shiny boots

The past is gone and it's just cold.

Zhivago

February 19

The more suns there are in the sky, the colder the air is. This morning there were five suns in the sky. At night I went to Inga's flat to warm up after walking the dog. She gave me some olive oil to rub on my cracked cheeks. She sat on the floor in her big white boots and threw empty cans at the walls. With each throw she looked more and more like an excited child in front of a puddle. I was surprised when she said she felt we might be getting a little sad this winter. We had planned to be happy until she left. We had already agreed to stay like two red fruits bobbing high above the forest floor. But we were both becoming like in last winter, like in the winter before. We were being carried off into rats' nests each evening, we were fizzing in someone else's paws. I felt the wasps devouring me even in summer.

Mid-February and the wealthier half of town has flown to Sedona I think. Or they're on the coast in Mexico. They're taking boats out to white cliffs. I'd love to feel the sun on me. Yet George Monbiot says there's no flying unless you believe these activities are 'worth the sacrifice of the biosphere and the lives of the poor'. That's true. Well yes that's true and so I must make time move through small experiences. I must curl a loose strand of hair around my finger and say, 'My life is as small or as big as I imagine it to be.' I must say, 'I only need to see my mother my father and brothers once a year.' I must love my night breath that has curled into frost flowers on the insides of the morning window. I must love these filigree feathers on the pane. I must rub a circle of ice away with my fingertip and hold a tapered candle up to the frost if I'm to get by. Then who am I?

I'm Omar Sharif in a nightshirt. A lamp is casting a calm pool of yellow light on the sheets of paper behind him, behind me. And the blizzard outside is howling. And the wolves are howling too.

I know about *Doctor Zhivago* because it's my mum's favourite film. She can play the theme tune on the piano. They filmed the movie in 1965 in Soria. The lead actors were the most beautiful, the director the most famous. The pressure on the film crew was big. They had less than a year to shoot two decades of Russian history. Two months into filming, disaster struck. Spring had come early to the Spanish plain. Seven thousand daffodils, planted by hundreds of technicians, hatched too soon, like golden chicks.

I love to imagine it.

John Box, the set designer, hurrying the spring flowers back into storage.

Ana, recruited as a technician, bunking with Valentina, Camila, and Marcia.

They are delighted the flowers bloomed early, for this job pays two hundred and fifty pesetas a day, and now everything is behind they will definitely be asked to stay for longer. Yes this job is pretty good! The canteen food is not bad—in the evenings there is always a cake decorated with oranges. The girls wrap extra slices in napkins. In the mornings they eat it in bed for breakfast.

While replanting the daffodils in April, they are laughing. While pouring powdered marble over vast white sheets of plastic so the green fields looked covered in snow, they are still laughing.

They must have done a good job at their assigned tasks. For Box's assistant has decided they can stay as back-up technicians until the end of summer. They are not surprised. He knows they need the money.

In the summer heat, they unroll hundreds of cling film rolls. They wrap chandeliers and furniture into fantastic shapes. They spray white hot wax over those wrapped chairs and on the dacha windows. They pour cold water quickly, quickly, until huge icicles form and gleam. They brush marble dust atop the scene so it shimmers. Several of the other workers develop coughs. Now the women are told they must wear two masks while working. Ana, Valentina, Camila, and Marcia get on with tossing crushed aspirin and soap flakes upon the wooden floor. They watch Omar and Julie slip about in fur coats like wax figures.

Summer turns to early autumn. The workers change from shorts into trousers. In the cool nights, once the others have begun to dream, Ana lies awake. She eats bits of cake. She thinks about snow.

She thinks about snow until she can think of nothing else.

Last week, on her afternoon off, she went to the travel agency in town. The woman behind the desk listened to Ana's wintery vision. She tapped her pen against the desk, then she brought out a map. She drew a short line across a blue oval near the top of Europe. She said, 'Getting to the Soviet Union—I don't think that will happen for you. But look how these cities are practically touching? It wasn't long ago that Finland was a Grand Duchy of Russia. Helsinki and St. Petersburg—they're practically sisters.'

'Have you been to Helsinki then?' Ana asked.

'Why would I go there?' the woman said. 'Look, you'll get your snow.'

Ana handed over a third of her money, and now her trip was officially set. She would go to Finland.

She was not the only one with plans.
All of Ana's bunkmates were going somewhere.

Camila to Santorini.
Valentina to the Sinai.
Marcia to her aunt's house outside Granada.

Their time on set was coming to a close. They were sitting drinking on the steps in town.

Camila was talking about how she was planning to travel forever. Valentina was growing very excited by the idea. She was sliding down the railings, singing,

'We are the gypsies
We are the wanderers
We are the rainbows of the sky!'

Marcia gave Valentina a look.

'Just because I'm happy,' Valentina said, glaring back.

'She's just happy,' Camila said. 'Look, there have been two types of people since Stone Age times. There are the majority, who are quite happy to stay home. They accept the status quo and live with the rest of the tribe. Then there are a few who are compelled to take risks. They seek out new and dangerous opportunities. They might make discoveries that benefit everyone. And what a good time they'll have, finding new mates and fruits to dine on! Anyway, they *must* travel. It's not possible for them to be happy staying at home. It just is what it is, Marcia.'

Marcia said, 'You can tell yourself whatever you want, Camila. You can wear all the bangles you like, Valentina. You can fill your head with sleighs and nonsense, Ana. But you are all just dreaming.'

'I just think we're lucky to be seeing a novel come to life,' Ana replied.

'We're not lucky, Ana. The director chose Soria because we're cheap workers. At some point you're going to come back home. You're all going to come back, you can't just travel forever. Go and see your mothers. Go and see your grandmothers.'

In September 1965, a skeleton crew has gone to Lake Louise in the Canadian Rockies to film the final scenes—moving images of real snow.

Ana is off on her own trip. A changing series of train attendants has been announcing stops as she travels. The names of the first places give feelings of warmth—Barcelona, Montpellier, Girona. Then feelings of cold—Bern, Warsaw, Tallinn.

Outside Helsinki station, a noticeboard lists various places for rent. The only room she can afford sits in a sea of mud.

Ana goes for long walks each day. She plays with the coins in her pocket, imagining they're roubles. She waits for snow.

Now the first snow of the year has come. She buys slices of cheesecake from the women outside the station. She watches housewives go about their tasks in sturdy dresses. She eats apples.

Snowflakes in Helsinki; she is definitely judging the way they disappear instantly on the pavement. She is definitely judging the people on the buses who look like sick animals in their furry hats. She'd hoped they'd look more like Lara.

At the start of the week, Ana mimed at her landlady for some extra blankets.

For three days now Ana has stayed in her room eating crackers and jam.

The landlady's daughter knocked on the door this morning. She said her mother would bring her up some dinner, but if Ana was looking to get some hot meals cheaply, she could try the university canteen a few streets away?

The canteen was on the top floor of the university's main campus building. Ana liked it there. A butter bun was only fifteen markka. And one customer wore a beauty spot and a red tasselled skirt.

Ana must have looked at the woman a little too intently, because after an hour she came over and sat down in the chair opposite her. She reached out to touch Ana's book on the table and said, '*¿Esto es trabajo escolar?*'

'You speak Spanish?' Ana replied.

The woman shrugged and said, 'Why wouldn't I?'

'Aren't you Finnish? Anyway it's not schoolwork. It used to be. Now I'm just reading for fun.'

'You're reading Schopenhauer for fun?'

'I find him very fun.'

'You know he didn't have such an easy life? All the neighbourhood children teased him over his loneliness. They chased after him and his poodle Atma as they walked down the street. They called her Mrs. Schopenhauer. He really could get no peace.'

'You're a student here?' Ana asked.

'I clean rooms across the square,' the woman replied, pointing out the window. 'I'm Hannele by the way. And it's a music school, the place I clean. But I'm going to Buenos Aires next year. They have the best dance schools in the world there. But tell me, why are you here? You didn't come to Helsinki to meet happy people. So what was it?'

Ana looked down at her lap. She said, 'All year I was working with pretend snow. I came here to see the real thing.'

'You're not going to see anything here but slush and turds,' Hannele replied. She got up then and talked with one of the women in the kitchen. She came back with a small silver dish filled with some kind of cream.

'Try this,' Hannele said.

Ana stuck a spoon in and sucked. Waves of heat rimmed her nostrils. Her eyes burned and watered.

Hannele spooned some of the sauce into her own mouth and winced. 'Your nose is going to burn just like that when you breathe up there, okay? Your cheeks, your lips—they're going to burn with every single breath.'

'When I breathe up where?' Ana asked.

'My aunt has a cabin up in the forest near Helvetinjärvi, so we'll go this weekend. She's been wanting me to go and check in on it anyway. But know this—every breath, every single breath in the cold is going to hurt. You're going to feel like you're eating horseradish all day long.'

On the train, Ana wondered if it was strange to be going off with someone she'd only just met. She would never do such a thing at home. Yet it didn't feel strange, being here on the train. It felt right, seeing trees and snowy fields dusted with chimney soot from the village houses. She wished Marcia could know the feeling. Of shaking with the movement of the carriage. Of something inside shaking too.

Hannele was reading Ana's book. She was saying that people thought Schopenhauer was a pessimist because he spoke of suffering. Yet she did not see it that way. She felt he was an optimist. For between the pendulum swings of pain and suffering, he pointed towards still points: moments of awe that released a person from the state of boredom, from the terrors of ambition. She lived for those moments, she said. For the feeling of standing on a summit and looking out at waves of mountains collapsing in the distance.

'For the feeling of being on the train with someone new,' Ana nodded.

'I don't think that's quite what Schopenhauer meant,' Hannele replied. 'But then he had difficulty with human relationships. His own mother told him as a teenager that she didn't want to spend time with him. He was just not fun to be around. He was much too clever and argumentative for his own good. And so he lived quite a solitary life. He'd rise early and take a cold sponge bath; he'd write and play a little flute. He'd eat out for lunch then take a nap and go for a walk with the dog. That's not such a stressful life. If anyone had the mental space to lose themselves in the surrounding landscape, it was him. Perhaps that was why he saw awe in places rather than people. Facing something as vast as a mountain, he felt that we humans suddenly feel a sense of our own smallness against its magnitude. As we reflect on that feeling, we begin to feel something else—we feel we *belong* to the mountain. In a way we *are* the mountain. We are a part of its vastness. That feeling of belonging is the opposite of self-centredness. And that's where momentary relief comes from when we contemplate awe in a landscape. Finally we can forget our selves. Finally we belong to the world.'

'In the canteen when we met,' Ana said, 'I was meant to be reading my book, but instead I noticed you. Perhaps everything has a cloud that wants to be noticed? These clouds want to join each other. And now here we are, together, in this carriage. Doesn't that carry the feeling of awe? When everything feels unfamiliar, I experience the world like a newborn. I'm absorbed and delighted by everything that catches my eye, and so I don't feel separate from what I see. That's such a good feeling. When I first went to Soria, the plain made me feel that way. The plain made me feel new. The mountains in the distance too. Yet the longer I spent there, the more the landscape seemed invisible to me. It became separate from me. I don't know why the feeling of awe fades. Already I am feeling a little used to this snow falling out the window,' Ana said, looking out.

'You didn't come to Finland for snow.'

'I did.'

'You didn't.'

'In a way I did. But I know I can't just keep on chasing unfamiliar things all my life.'

'I extend the feeling of awe by dancing,' Hannele said. 'I feel the mountains inside me when I move. When you go back to Spain, I will dance and remember you.'

'I wish I could dance,' Ana said.

'You'll find something.'

'I can't sing or write.'

A daytime owl flew past the train window.

'Maybe I could draw owls?'

'That owl does not want to be made cute,' Hannele said.

'That owl is so serious,' Ana replied, nodding.

The women got off at the platform. They walked through the woods to the cabin. The windows were covered with ice. Ana rubbed a circle from the pane. As she did, she felt wolves flickering.

Hannele said they should go outside before dark.

They went out in their coats. They lay like small bears in the snow.

'Each snowflake on the ground contains a little piece of pollen or dust or spore at its heart,' Hannele said. 'Each snowflake is a sort of flower, with a seed at its centre. This is why the air looks and feels so clear and fresh here—all the pollen and dust that was floating about in the air all summer is now caught in the centre of each snowflake covering the ground.'

——

Soft flakes continued to land on their coats like jewels. There were very fine shapes among them—ferny crystals, pillars and prisms.

Hannele said a man named Johannes Kepler was once the German court mathematician to the Holy Roman Emperor Rudolf II. In 1611 he made a single booklet titled *Strena seu de nive sexangula.* The introduction began with a scene harking back to a winter's day when, on crossing the Charles Bridge in Prague, he noticed snowflakes falling on his coat. He came to ponder their exceptional geometry.

He contrasted the sixfold symmetry of snowflakes to the similar symmetries found in flowers. He decided that such similarities were in appearance only. For while flowers contained the stunning complexity exhibited in all living things, a snowflake, despite its sophisticated appearance, was a simple thing made from ice. Why then, would it take on such a delicate and beautiful shape?

Kepler decided God was being playful.

God was in the habit of playing with the passing moment.

'How do you know all this?' Ana asked.

'I think everyone knows this.'

Wolf

March 1

Sometimes I wonder if things would be different if this was a different kind of town. If there was a bakery full of morning buns and an old bookshop. If there was a sauna where men beat birch branches in the air till everyone was glowing on the benches like candles.

If there were trams streaming through rivers of wildflowers, I'd like that.

I must be thinking of Berlin again.
But I don't want to live in Berlin again.

March 5

Today I walked through the town—past the banks, the petrol stations, the pharmacies, the fudge shops—until I was on the other side.

I walked until the ice became soft snow. Everything was shining. When I placed one fist inside an indent of the prints I'd been following, it fit like a mitten.

There is only one animal whose paw matches my fist like a mitten.

I stroked the track into oblivion. I felt gold eyes blink back. A black tail rocking back and forth. My heart beating so fast.

Aroma

March 9

I've been walking through the darkness since six this morning. Walking with the tea lantern past the trailers, past the mansions. Into the woods. The light of this candle has been lighting the tree trunks gold.

Now there's a wood dog
Honey hound
Sharp fox

She's dropped down on her hind legs.
A warm wet redness spreads through my dress,
It's beautiful to watch her,
Rayed red and gold.

No lamb or rabbit in the white-cupped vale to protect
I can watch a fox without worry.

Such a strange time this is.
How beautiful it is.

Where's she turning now, why's she running down the hill? Fox, come on now.

Where are you going?

Fox, please, stay like you're in a painting.

At any other time, meeting a fox, even if only for a moment, would have bolstered me for days. But I've been in a filthy mood. These projects, they're not transforming a thing about me. They might suppress certain emotions for short periods, but those emotions then come bursting forth when I'm at my lowest ebb. When I'm nearing the end of my luteal phase, no amount of forced stoicism can hold my petulant nature back. Yet I so wish to be a Stoic. Annia Cornificia Faustina Minor was a great Stoic of the ancient world. She quietly severed her own veins. Porcia Catonis was good at staying quiet too. She stabbed herself in the thigh to show how good she was at keeping secrets. I can't keep anything to myself.

All this metallic sadness spurting through my knuckles. I shouldn't have gone outside this morning without the puppy. How happy she seems as she skitters about the snow and digs up its surface. Always she favours her right paw for digging. After sending up shoots of snow and dirt beneath her claws, she pauses, then bends her damp muzzle into the fresh-turned earth. She dips her nose in; she inhales at length. Her tail wags faster, she bends in further.

Actually she seems quite happy anywhere. She'll dig into the sofa as though it's a snowbank; she'll play with a piece of baguette as though it's a mouse. But she is best at detecting subtle aromas. Using her fine sense of smell to read the stories of the forest must be satisfying to her. Moving through invisible clouds of scent flowing along the paths—the feeling must be as good for her as watching the sunrise is to me. Perhaps it is her sense of smell—so much better than mine—that makes her so delighted. Perhaps this world smells so much better than it looks. In any event, it's because of her placid nature that I know my current mood is not indicative of the actual state of the world. It is me that is dour and not the world. And so it is me that must change.

This week, for a project, I wondered about purchasing a sommelier training kit. I'm glad I did not buy one in the end. After all, it takes more creativity to not spend money than it does to earn it. And the dog has really been taking me to some excellent spots in the woods. Her ability to hunt out places where other animals have urinated, for example, is second to none. She's also found a lot of mouse holes by the bases of the trees; we've had a good time following their snow tracks in search of blood spots.

At the start of the week we lay in the abandoned daybeds of two elk. Looking across at her in her snow-shell, I could see her eyes shining with my reflection; I think she was watching her reflection shining in my eyes too.

This week we bent our noses deep into the moss. I was instantly a child running along the old wall again—a T-shirt tied round my head to look like Andre Agassi, green tufts flinging up with our trainers while rocks went tumbling down doocots towards spiders.

If I tore up those mosses and trod them into the carpet, could I evoke the feeling of running across trembling stone walls with my brothers again? Would I feel at home then?

The dog is content. She doesn't menstruate. Menstruation is rare among animals. Only us primates and one kind of mouse, one kind of shrew and a few bats experience it. I've read descriptions of these animals' behaviours. While the baboon is a famously social animal, just before her period she acts distant from others. She goes off alone to eat fruits and nuts by herself in a tree. I act similarly.

I shouldn't have gone out without the puppy. I shouldn't have gone out alone with all my emotions on the edge of my hairs; I felt them tingling as soon as I rose from the bed this morning.

It's not right to show dark emotions to the trees. Better to stay in and hide from myself. If only I had a proper medieval room where I could be quiet. That would be perfect. Just me and a piss pot and a weak fire.

It would be hard at first, being shut up in a cell. But I imagine that, after months or years of doing little other than praying, a lasting calmness would eventually descend upon me.

Of course, without real windows I'd likely become sun-deficient very quickly. And it'd be hard, eating bowls of watery brose only. Still, bodily deprivation might be worth it if it meant no more blood—no more scraps or red rags. I'd get really physically sick, shut up in the dark like that. I'd be shaking my teeth out on my knees.

One last tooth jangling in my mouth and my uterus quiet finally. I think I might not mind gumming cabbage if it meant no more periods. I suppose it's wrong to think that. It would just be a treat to live without self-pity as part of my monthly make-up. Yes I could easily live with just a little hunger, just a little wounded mouth.

If I had woken the dog this morning, she would have come out with me and I would have been fine. But she was all tucked in beside him. So I went through to the other room. I switched on the light. I picked up my stockings and socks that were bunched on the carpet by the sofa. I put them on and waited for the kettle to boil. I filled a hot water bottle and cradled it. Then I switched off the light and fell into a filthy mood. Why'd he gone hogging the blanket all night?

All night the fox had been screaming outside the window. She was looking for mates. Why was she bothering?

It's just a little sad, the way these eggs keep leaving my body. They are so tiny to be going out into the world alone. Each one is so small, even smaller than the period at the end of a sentence.

These eggs that grew inside me while I was in my mother's womb.

Me coming from one of the eggs that grew in her while she lived inside my grandmother's womb.

It's a little sad to lose them. I'd like to lay them somewhere more beautiful than in a toilet bowl. I'd like to stop thinking about my mother.

Cougar

March 16

Last week, I could not bring myself to bake an apple. Today I feel nested in light, walking the dog beside the beaver lodge.

Crystals in the air and all this silken snow beneath us reminds me of a sewn-closed sleeve that's long been unravelling. All the smallest animals climbed inside it months ago. The worms and frogs, the mice and voles. All season, foxes and other animals have been tearing up winter's sleeve and collecting them. By the creek right now, on the snow there is so much blood. A fox did not do that. A cougar has been eating a deer there. Now there are signs on the edge of town asking the townspeople to exercise caution, to keep an eye on their dogs and children.

I can't believe I live among lions. Too long here and I still can't believe it. Sun cats feasting on stumbled deer. Silent hunters following the wake of hooves. I'm not so scared. If I had children, I would be scared. Inga had a classmate attacked by a cougar when she was a child. Still, it's good to prepare for every eventuality. After all, I could easily come across a young and cocky one, or a sick one that has become too slow to catch cold rabbits. A desperate one like that might well lunge at my neck while I'm looking for rocks.

It won't know I've been preparing my reflexes for such a moment.

I'm preparing right now.

I'm here to practise throwing things and screaming in a place where I can't be heard by other humans. I'll scream and imagine green eyes flashing. I'll skim a stone towards black lips parting.

Only now I'm actually looking for rocks instead of just talking to myself, I'm realising of course they're all frozen in place. Today there are three suns, and beneath the bases of the trees where the winds have blown the snow away the rocks are frozen. They're frozen beneath the deep snow on the edge of the pond; they're frozen beneath the mice and the frogs they're frozen frozen frozen and my hands are like icy slabs as I try to release one.

I know what to do.

My flask of tea has been chiming like a temple bell against the buckle on my backpack ever since I got here. I'll throw it. I'll throw it at a golden back turning—at a tail flicking like rope then shortening to string.

Spring

Bear

March 30

Perhaps I am making myself sound tough with all this talk of throwing things at imaginary lions. I know I'm not. Now the sun is shining and the snow is melting and the bears are waking, I'm often scared.

It wasn't like this when I first got here. I used to go looking for bears on my bike. There was that big tousled one in the verge. His long claws scraped up dandelions that warm evening. His eyes met mine, then slid back to the flowers.

Then I read that book about the bear who opened up a woman's skull like a lid on a tub of ice cream. The bear started to eat her while she was still conscious. She survived, but she was physically and emotionally devastated. She took her own life a few years later.

I often imagine being pinned to the forest floor by a grinning bear. She's tipped my nose towards her musty crotch. My eyelids are blinking in terrified rhythm as she prizes open my cranium. As her long, warm tongue goes lapping at creamy brain tendrils, juices run from her saffron claws. Furred fists plunge in, and plunge in, and plunge in. She's having the time of her life.

One last flinch of my big toe.
And she wanders on, leaving red prints along the path.
She's found later by the wardens, her pelt still wet.
Walkie-talkies bristle.
Then there are two bodies dead.

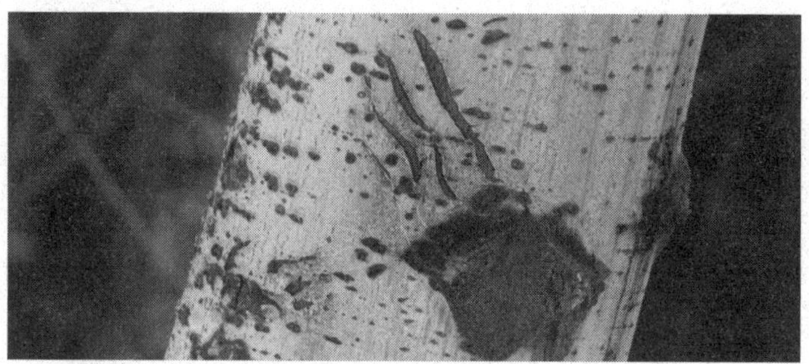

I know attacks from bears are very rare. Something could happen, but I'm much more likely to have my guts smacked into the road by a car.

Yes a black bear dragged a sausage dog into these woods last week, but it's still rare.

Anyway, I know where the grizzlies are at this time of year. They're hanging out on the train tracks. They're eating spilled grain while waiting for the first flowers to come up. They're pawing ladybirds and ants. Then as soon as the flowers start to bloom, they follow spring up to the highest meadows. I don't know anyone who loves flowers as much as a brown bear.

Today I saw one small brown bear. Then another. They looked about two or three years old. They had dark moons beneath their eyes. They were siblings, but I couldn't see their mother. She must have kicked them out of the den. They were coming right towards me. They were ambling quite peacefully as I crawled, shaking, up to the nearest rocky patch. If I was living a few generations ago, I would have thought the *fath fith* incantation I'd said before going out had rendered me invisible to their predatory eyes. As things stood, I hadn't made a single divination.

I really respect Charlie Russell and Maureen Enns. They spent years in Kamchatka raising orphaned grizzly cubs. To begin with, she was a little more afraid about living in deep Russia than he was. But Maureen soon grew used to their little cabin surrounded by volcanoes and animals. She liked to sit amid the flattened grasses where the grizzlies had slept. Then she'd paint landscapes from a bear's eye view.

While in Russia, the pair of them read a book called *Exploration of Kamchatka 1735–1741*. In it, a young geographer named Stepan Krasheninnikov described meeting Koryak men who had been 'frayed' a bit by the brown bears. He believed the bears knew they were hunters. Bears are extremely smart—their intelligence compares with that of higher primates, and these ones really didn't like hunters. The women, who did not hunt, were never attacked. During berry season, the bears would follow the foraging girls around like domestic dogs.

The bears seemed to have moral codes understood by the Koryak. If a family was leaving their wood cabin for a time, they would leave an elderly female family member inside. Not because old women were superfluous. It was just known that a bear would never attack an old woman—not even for jam.

Maureen and Charlie loved Russia's bears. Still, they always carried bear spray.

I always carry bear spray. I've never had to use it, still I'm always pulling off the glow-in-the-dark safety cap. I practise swooping the spray through the air so I have the necessary moves if the time comes. And still I'm most scared at this time of year. As the winter nights piled up, bears grew into phantoms in my mind. Yet who is benefiting from my fears?

A few years before Charlie Russell died, I watched him give a talk. His voice was gentle and his hair was white and pulled this way and that. He wore Gloria Steinem glasses and there was something entrancing about the way he viewed the world. 'You don't need to hoot and holler to let bears know you're coming along the path,' he said to the audience. 'That will just scare all the birds and other animals away. Bears have such good hearing. They move out of the way for each other just by listening out for the sounds of twigs snapping. When I go for a walk, I just pick up a nice branch near the start of the trail. I break off pieces as I go, I have a wonderful time. I meet so many birds.'

This week I have been picking up twigs. I have been breaking them. I have been having a wonderful time.

Loupe

April 1

I get jealous of everyone at home during this time of year. I imagine them amid the bluebells and streams and I look out at the mud and the dusty bottles around my apartment building and think, what a stupid place I came to. How stupid I am to have come here. I had everything but romantic love. Now I only have romantic love and it's not enough.

At this time of year, I know it's better if I don't look outside too much. It's getting browner all the time as the snow melts, as the soil falls in the rivers. And while I do like brown—brown being the colour of hiding and skin and freckles and female birds and stairways and teeth and cocoa and kimonos and baby beavers coming out of winter's second womb—I really hate seeing those hungry animals at this time of year. All those elk eating the bark while their eye-whites roll are hungry; the squirrels are hungry, the birds are hungry, I hate to see it. So I've been staying in with my loupe. When I use it, I feel like a different animal. I can look up close at the woven needles of a cedar branch on the table and see they're braided like my niece's hair. And the pine cone on the table has nipples. It's heaving with breasts on breasts.

The spider's sac on the wall, it's as grey and small as a tac. I pierced its silk fibres with my fingernail just now. Now tiny eggs are glowing amid the candlelight. Spider caviar. They're going nowhere either.

Rock

April 9

The air's getting warmer. The rocks that were frozen in place are sliding down the hillsides. Beneath the trees, if I bend down and grip the smallest rocks, they're moving up, up, into my pocket.

I could go to all the sheltered spots in the woods now.

I could pick up rocks and take them home. In a mortar and pestle I could grind them up. By suspending pink rock dust in egg yolks or animal fat, it's possible to paint anything. Paper. Clay. Moons. The domed roofs of caves. If I paint my skin with rock pigments, there'll be two million years on my hands. Three million. Four. I think I'll do this. I think what I have to believe in is playing with each passing moment.

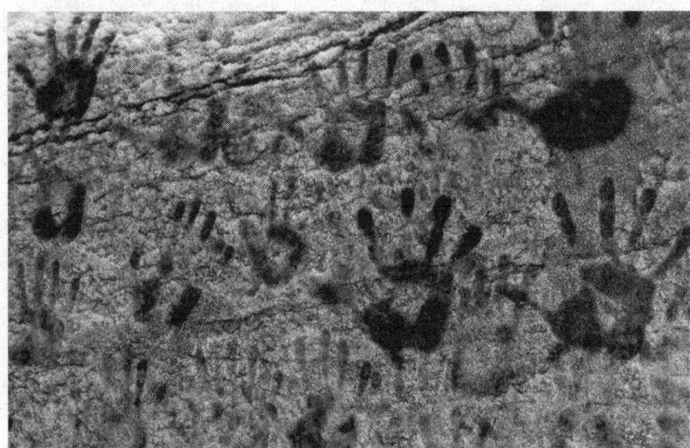

Path

April 18

When he came home from work, he found me in a state by the window. He listened to my lamentations. Then he began to tell me a story.

'A woman is coming across a beautiful garden. It's very lush. There is a pear tree laden with fruit. How beautiful it is! Then a bear comes lolloping in. It's shaking the pear tree until the fruits fall, it's kicking the fruit to pulp for no reason. It's devouring the plants, it's defecating everywhere.'

'That bad bear!' I said.

He pulled my arms down, gently, and said, 'You may be the bear.'

Well I was feeling sick, wasn't I. I was feeling sorry for myself. The surface of my tongue was braided with rough white fur. All day I'd been bored, gargling salt water and nursing my mouth ulcers. I'd been feeling strange all day. Watching black dogs galloping past the window, I'd been in a right state. Doing kitten work while fever-sweats poured from my skin, I'd been sure this sickness would feel different in a different place. If I was rocking in a wooden chair in woollen tights, this sickness would feel peaceful because I would be peaceful. If I was in my dream house, I could accept every state.

I can see my dream house completely. I've seen it a thousand times.

Flames are leaping about the hearth. Smoke is curling through the room, across the egg yolk, the candle, it's drifting across the table, across the sugar bowl lacquered red and gold; smoke is touching the windowsill, there. It's lying upon the cow's tooth and the comb, it's drifting over the bed and dresser and flagstone floor, it's rising through beams and rafters, out through thatch and into bright new air. It's drifting above the linen, above the woman fanning the leaves, it's spinning towards the water meadows, the hazel trees, the weaving geese—into their song it's spinning, it's coasting into clouds where it's given shoes and a new name.

Sometimes he is in this dream beside me and sometimes he is not.
I wish he was always in this dream,
Where there are iron handles and lace curtains,
Where we're happy.

I used to love being sick, just a bit sick, with all my family taking turns to check in on me. Soft steps coming up the stairs, the iron latch opening on the old door, and one brother's face appearing, then the other. A warm hand touching my damp forehead. A hand stroking my hair. A lamp shaped like a glass tulip above.

Between the work hours I've been sitting in the bath and chewing on the razor handle. Even in here Wayne's cigarette smoke has been leaching through the wall vents. Before that, to make time move faster I was watching films.

From watching *Les glaneurs et la glaneuse*, I learned that the practice of gleaning has not ended in France. People there are still bending in fields. In 2000, the filmmaker Agnès Varda filmed them in action.

She met a family of Travellers living in a caravan.

Even though they were living in an unloved spot beside a busy road, not harming anyone, people did not like them being there. They were being threatened with evacuation by the local authorities.

Nearby, in another group of caravans, was a group of men. They were dealing with alcoholism. The air by now was cold and damp, blue shadows were lengthening. It was scary for them. Varda talked with these people whose financial worries were very real. Millions in this wealthy country were living in poverty.

She went into towns where tensions were erupting. She met anti-consumerist activists fighting supermarket managers who poured bleach on the fresh bread that was tossed in skips at the end of the day.

She filmed people for whom gleaning was a simple form of joy—they did it to be close to their childhood memories. She met one Michelin-starred chef who was gleaning leftover grapes from the local vineyards. He said the practice reminded him of being out with his grandparents. His eyes looked gentle as he spoke of them.

She interviewed a lawyer in a cabbage field. He read out France's gleaning law from 1554. It stated that 'the poor, the wretched, the deprived' can take what they need after the harvest.

That lawyer noted that while many gleaners today can afford to go to the supermarket, this did not change their legal situation.

These people who were gleaning for fun had a need too.

'There is a need for fun,' he said.

Varda filmed herself. She filmed the mould that had grown on her ceiling in the shape of a heart. She filmed heart-shaped potatoes left in the fields to turn poisonous green. She took them home so they could grow arms. She held these potatoes she loved up to the camera. They looked like they wanted to touch everyone. When she was holding the camera, this was how they looked.

She seemed to say, look at everything. These people you pass by on the street, those caravans you drive past. Look.

Agnès Varda seemed to see something special in everyone she met. She became especially interested in a man who she'd noticed gleaning vegetables at her local market in Paris. He had a strong, upright body and large brown eyes. She watched him rifling through produce boxes at the end of the day. Eventually they got to talking. Once he warmed to Varda, he described the specific nutritional qualities of parsley. How did he know about that? she asked. He had a master's in biology.

His name was Alain F. He sold newspapers outside a busy train station. The commuters appeared to be largely disinterested in him—and even repulsed by his lowly status.

This Alain F

For much of the day, he lived in a wide and silent plane of his own making. He gleaned herbs and sold a few papers to commuters who did not look him in the eye. Then he rode the train to a high-rise building on the outskirts of Paris. He lived in a small flat there. He spent his evenings volunteering down in the basement.

He'd set up a classroom to teach French to people who'd recently arrived from Mali. At night, among these students, he experienced an atmosphere of comradery, friendship, and respect.

I love Alain F. I've only met one other person who's eschewed the trappings of status so entirely.

I met him years ago, near Fukuoka train station. His hair was completely white. He was wearing surfer shorts and putting flowers in my backpack while I peered down at my map after getting off the ferry from Korea. He spoke only a few words of English, and I spoke only a few words of Japanese. Still, we could communicate. He called himself Navigator. Actually he was shouting *Navigator!* Over and over. I don't think he was mad, though the people around us were looking at us like he was mad.

I felt ashamed to be seen with him as he steered me to the bus station. He waved as the bus pulled out; he was smiling and pumping his fists in the air. He had only been kind to me. And I'd been so filled with shame throughout our interaction.

A few days later, from a distance I watched Navigator filling up his arms with leftover bread and cakes from various sellers at the market outside the station. He was trying to share the goods with commuters. Most dodged to avoid him. Then a handsome man in a Patagonia jacket joined him. They went round the last of the stalls. They handed out the rest of the produce together. I went up to talk with them. Navigator's friend said that Navigator slept on the street. He moved to a new city every few weeks. In each place, he did the same thing. He took what was about to be thrown away by florists, by market sellers—and he shared it with others.

I like to think of Navigator as a man who made the sane choice to act according to his core beliefs. I am so far from being this way.

I was walking the dog to the creek this morning, ulcers burning my mouth, when I heard shouting coming from behind me. I turned around and saw a tall man. His eyes were flashing with hate as he shouted that where I was walking was not a path.

I said it looked like a path.

He said the gap between his house and the neighbour's was a utility access point—had I not heard of such a thing? Was I dumb or something?

He stood and stared at me for a long time. He said he'd noticed me photographing the birds in the trees. The neighbour was going to cut those trees down, so I'd stop coming.

I said no one had to cut down the trees. They didn't need to be doing that.

I stumbled back to the flat via the creek. I felt my unbrushed teeth and the hairs on the backs of my knees as I went. All those million-dollar houses running up and down the water.

I was growing more and more upset with them. Just what was he on about? It's not a path? Everything's a path. You can walk wherever you like. At home you can. Pretty much wherever the fishwives walked, you can walk. All over the fields and along the lanes. Walk and walk, that's your right. And if you have an old rowan tree on your property, you'll never cut it down. Someone planted it to ward off evil spirits ages ago; you won't just cut it down.

Of course some of the farmers put padlocks and barbed wire around their fences despite the right to roam, and Duncan

Drummond did tell you as a kid he had a mind to call the police on you for being in his field. But that just wasn't true, was it. He knew it wasn't true and you knew too. For even though you were quite small, eight or nine, Mum had already given you a lesson on your legal rights. Still, you were shaking as Duncan Drummond spoke, you were shaking then and you're shaking now.

In Scotland it's legal to walk and camp pretty much wherever—so long as no one can see your tent from their living room window and you're not bothering the cows or sheep, you can go and eat your pig nuts wherever you like.

Some folk in the past must have worked hard to open up public access like that—it can't have been easy to convince the powerful.

I think a swath of the English country rejoiced when Madonna and Guy Ritchie's barrister failed to make the case that his clients' human rights were being violated by the general public's right to wander on their estate land near Devon. Challenging the core of the Countryside and Rights of Way Act like that. What a thing to do. What a thing, when already walkers down south have a miserable lot. Already they can hardly walk or camp anywhere.

Now I'm being told I can't even walk the shortcut to the creek? Can't walk on unfenced grasses. Can't eat berries.

I'll sit outside their houses among tufts of black bombazine if they so much as think about cutting down the rowans. It doesn't take much for the trowe in me to start peering through my roots. She'll show them they're up to something worth mourning.

Threatening to cut down the trees. Suppose I must really have been disturbing them.

Day after day, look at her—ruining the grass with her mucky feet . . .

Didn't pay a million dollars to have the grass trampled on. Worked bloody hard for your privacy, and still you have to deal with bloody women stomping about your land. Well you're not taking it anymore—you'll give her a piece of your mind.

Maybe that man was upset because, as a child, there had been debt collectors at the door. They'd skirted round his family home and peered up the path—it scared him then and the memories scare him now. So no he doesn't like seeing strangers sidling up the path, it makes him start to shake actually.

Or perhaps I was the last straw. Perhaps he just got bad news I cannot conceive of and I was the last straw.

But that's not the most likely thing. The most likely thing is that he very much believes land can be owned. Given that being rich and owning property is so esteemed, it's likely he would value wealth and property above many things.

Ambient values shape us, they do. They've shaped me—such that there's often friction between my surface thoughts and my deeper, romantic belief in the essential goodness and beauty beneath the core of all things. This leads to the terrible sense of alienation I feel within my own self.

April 19

This evening, in the bath, I was reading *The Marriage of Heaven and Hell* when a single line struck me.

'*Shame is Pride's cloak.*'

Shame is Pride's cloak.

If I am feeling shame, it is because I am full of pride.

My shame on being told off by the neighbour said little about him, and much about my sense of pride, and how I hurt when it's dented.

If I am to become more like Navigator and Alain F, which is what I want, then I must lose my sense of shame—which is a kind of pride.

I will do this by inviting opportunities that force me into a state of humility. Yes, I'll break shame's form by inviting in shameful moments until they no longer affect me.

Of course, on coming to such a conclusion I have been feeling quite puffed-up.

Birch

April 28

This week, a neighbour shouted at me while I was picking up birch branches that had come sweeping down the alley with the storm.

It was perfect. He'd love to have known. I was taking the branches so I could beat myself in the shower.

Land

April 31

This week I received an email from the Park. It said the land where I'd been walking was not private property—it was municipal land and as such was free for any member of the public to walk on.

It's not municipal land. It's plant and animal land. It's Indigenous land. And I no longer feel like walking there.

Dew

May 1

My father says that, on the first morning in May, Orkney girls would go rubbing their faces in dew so their complexion would be beautifully clear for the rest of the year.

There's no dew in the mountains at this time of year, only frost, but I've not been feeling sorry for myself.

This morning I went to the creek and tipped my head in the water. I wasn't breaking shame's form by doing this. It was only invigorating, seeing the creek as a loupe with its sand magnified.

Before long I was imagining the unwed girls of Stromness waiting outside the bakery over a century ago;

Isla Grace Sophie Mhairi Ann Freya Lucy Catriona Ruby Fiona
Hilda and Sorcha were waiting on Ingibjorg.

Hilda was saying it was too bloody early for all this,
Mhairi was impatiently tapping her feet on flagstone,
Ruby said she felt so tired she was going to spew—

Then Sorcha nudged Hilda and said *here Ingy comes*.

Freya called out that she could see Ingibjorg's nightdress.
Ingibjorg sidled up to Freya—
She whispered *you bitch* while laughing through tiny teeth.

The girls went up the hill in pairs.
The only person up at that hour was John Brown on his postal round.

Mhairi stopped to watch him,
Then Ann tugged her sleeve and said *later*.

They rushed up the streets in twos and threes.
It took them forever to reach Brinkie's Brae because—
Ruby had to stop to pick some primroses from Tommie's pots,
And Fiona spent at least a minute with Fish and Mist the cats tucked beneath her dress,
Then Ann was doing the same with Chip.

Hilda paused to watch the starlings,
Then Sorcha was leaning over the railings with what she said was a stitch.

So that by the time the girls reached the hill, the morning sun was already rising over the herring boats plying stillest water.

Ingibjorg bent down on the hill and swiped her hands through the dewy grass. She touched her temples, her chin and eyelids. Then the others did the same. They laced their lips with water.

They sat down on the grass and closed their eyes.

Behind her eyelids Freya saw depthless swirling

Isla saw poppies moving in violet fields

Grace, the doctor's daughter, said, with their eyes closed, they were actually seeing inside their own bodies. They were viewing sunlight as it passed through their blood, as it flowed across their eyelids.

Well, Ingibjorg could swear she only saw peedie white worms.

The girls stayed quiet for a moment,
Then burst out laughing.

Grace laughed too. 'No,' she said. 'Those are white blood cells. Those peedie white worms are your own cells. They're pulsing in time with the beating of your heart.'

The girls watched their hearts beating behind their eyelids.

Then Ruby opened her eyes and said, 'The men down there; they think we're up here trying to get bonny for them.'

The laughter of every girl was beating the air like drums then. The girls were blasting the boats out to Greenland.

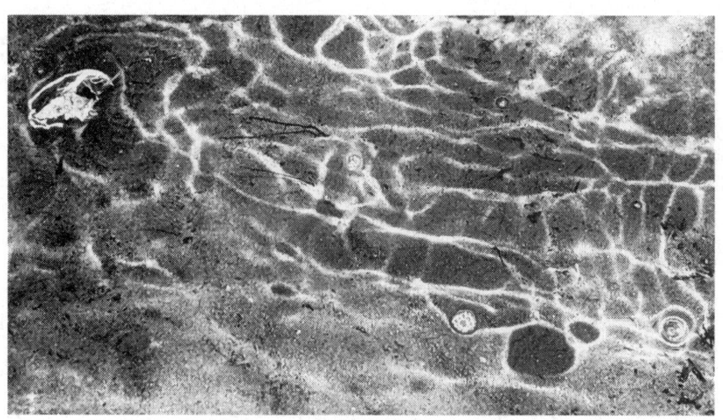

This week I closed my eyes in the sun. When I opened my eyes, I watched dark circles flowing along the sand on the stream bottom. Circles tumbled like black moons down the sun-bright bed. They appeared and disappeared like bright rings of light haloing dark curled otters.

What sends those dark spots flowing across the shallows?

If I place my thumb upon the surface of the water, I can create them.

Communion

May 7

In the tree across the street tonight, Inga and I saw an animal. It was the size of a pencil case but it looked like a kitten.

The town seamstress walked by with her doodle. She said *they're little jerks*.

Inga said *they're not little jerks*.

We knelt on the pavement.

The marten flashed its pink tongue at us like a wafer.

It flashed us. And flashed us. And flashed us again.

Dandelion

May 10

There's a lot you can do with birches at this time of year. You can secretly make a small nick, that's one trick. Make a nick in the bark, then drink its spring juices like a calf with her cow.

Place a handful of sticky buds—a few and no more from each tree—in a small bottle of vodka. In a matter of days, the astringent, clear liquid will turn dark and sweet.

There are rhubarb nubbins rising from the earth like knuckles now. Once stalks come, you can lace them with honey and eat them raw.

There are dandelions on the south sides of the streets.
Lion's tooth, pissinlit, piss-in-bed, priest's crown, puffball, swine's snout, telltime, yellow gowan, dent-de-lion, tarashaquq.
In a few weeks they'll look like owlets stirring.

Once I went for a walk with a man named Gord who liked to tap all the trees with owl holes in them. He must have knocked on thousands of trees over the years.

How many times had he seen a bird on knocking?

Not once. But every time he went knocking, behind his eyes an image came to mind of feathers blowing like dandelion clocks. And that's why he knocked on trees.

Morel

May 12

Now the springtime mushrooms are popping up, I've messaged the superintendent about the gleaning laws in France. I have suggested that here, too, there is a need for fun.

The poet Friedrich Schiller said if you're to have a beautiful soul, then you must experience joy—for goodness and morality are not to be worked at, but come through dedication to art and play.

These morels popping up now look like pine cones. These fine little wood tulips, they're just asking to be picked.

Someone in Kyrgyzstan, or in the green of Siberia, will be plucking a few from the ground.

They'll have their old sayings for when to find them.

When the leaves are the size of a mouse's ear.
When the trees are covered in buds.

Nose to stalk, these mushrooms smell tender, like wet almonds. Yellow constellations dust the honeycomb of each cap. If I take one for a walk to my kitchen, I can disperse those spores with my shaking. I feel I'm meant to.

The first fungi looked like smooth, armless saguaro. They grew up to two storeys tall. The world four hundred million years ago was hostile. On the land there were only small plants and animals. But those giant mushrooms did not need much. For sustenance, they mined rocks. As the minerals in the stones were released into the earth, soil was formed. Gradually it became rich enough to support the growth of big, lush plants. Those big plants released oxygen into the air, and eventually the planet became habitable for lynx, and hares, and us.

How else to say thank you but to shake today's spores into the air?

I want to write more letters. I want to ask the superintendent why he is permitting the felling of the aspens behind our flats. Their trunks appear dark green in winter, then bone white in summer. They have dark eyes running up them where branches fell on receiving too little sunlight. Those eyes. I've never seen an evil look in a single one.

There are marks in the bark from bear cubs that practised climbing here generations ago. It would be a shame to lose those stories to the sky.

Still, the landlord's workers are wrapping new plastic ribbons around those trunks after I pull them down each night. I've looked at the rules and the only thing that could stop the culling would be travelling birds nesting in them.

Anna's hummingbirds have already stopped a section of pipeline construction further west from being completed. A group of birders must have followed their iridescence into the thickets. Saw thimble-sized nests formed from spiderwebs and plant-down. Knew of a law protecting such nesting places until autumn—started making calls.

Now those eggs will hatch. And the trees that contain these nests will have their summer.

All trees should have their summer.

They have endured such a long winter after all.

Letter

May 17

This week I got a letter. It stated, to all intents and purposes, there is no need for fun.

There is a need for fun.

Cat

May 18

Kris informed me in the shop just now that some cat owners in town are not happy with my latest letter. He said I should stop sending them. Did I not know they were being read out loud in all the town council meetings? Now the peace officer is fining everyone after they've received an initial warning.

'Everyone in town hates you—' Kris said.

I said I must send my letters. The birds cannot write. But I can write.

Kindling

May 24

I've finally found it. A poem to help me break shame's form. This one's as old as roots. I've been reading it for a while now.

Chants like this one, Hebridean though they are, were shaped in the deserts of the Middle East and North Africa. They began with the Desert Mothers and Fathers who withdrew from society and fled into the sandy wilderness in the third century. Those men and women lived in cells like bees, or alone up stone pillars. They were having all sorts of visions. I think it's from them that these words were fashioned.

I am kindling my fire this morning
In presence of the holy angels of heaven,
In presence of Ariel of the loveliest form,
In presence of Uriel of the myriad charms,
Without malice, without jealousy, without envy,
Without fear, without terror of any one under the sun,
But the Holy Son of God to shield me.

God, kindle Thou in my heart within
A flame of love to my neighbour,
To my foe, to my friend, to my kindred all,
To the brave, to the knave, to the thrall,
O Son of the loveliest Mary,
From the lowliest thing that liveth,
To the Name that is highest of all.

In my malice and envy, I travel in ancient company.

Togaidh mi mo theine an diugh,
An lathair athlean naomh nimh,
An lathair Airil is ailde cruth,
An lathair Uyiril nan uile sheikh,
Gun ghnu, gun tnu, gun fharmad.
Gun gniomh, gun gheimeh roimh beach fun ghrelin,
Ach Naomh Mhac De da m' thearmad.

Dhe fadaidh fein na m' chridhe steach,
Aingheal ghraidh do m' choimhearsnach,
Do m' namah, dhoom' dhaam, do m' chairde,
Do 'not-aoidh, don daoibh, do 'n traille.
A Mhic na Moire min-ghile,
Bho 'n ni is isde crannchaire,
Gu ruig an t-Ainm is airde.

What were the Desert Mothers and Fathers up to while the biblical canon as we know it was being set in Rome? Drinking water from goatskin bladders. Plucking herbs like birds. Pulling long bush roots from the sand and making fires to stay warm. Gardening. In the desert gardens they grew lotus blossoms, roses, jasmine, anemones, and chrysanthemums. They ate peaches and jujube in modest portions, for they felt that the fewer resources they used, the more there would be for others.

There in the desert they were creating their own version of Christianity. They were giving themselves over to asceticism and praying with devotion. They were praying all night and all day. What ideas were they forming as they did so?

Ideas of rejecting the formal self that exists among company.
Ideas of seeking a God they alone could find through prayer, rather than a stereotype formed by others.
Ideas of saving the world by saving oneself.

These ideas travelled beneath the surface of the dominant Christian ideology to peasant cultures all over Europe.

The movement of Desert Mothers and Fathers grew and grew. At some point there were tens of thousands of people encountering themselves in organised communities or alone as stylites. Many, I've read, were from poor backgrounds. Many, I've read, were women. Their stories we know little of, for the biographies of the poor and the female are rarely told. But the (surely apocryphal) story of Mary of Egypt has been passed on.

Mary walked across the River Jordan in the fourth century. She spent the next five decades all alone in the desert repenting.

All she had in the first weeks was three baguettes to talk to. They turned hard as stone in the heat.

She nibbled on them; she suffered greatly. At times the sun burned her up. At other times she shivered from the frost. Often she was falling to the ground. She was lying without breath and without motion. Or she was flinging herself on the sand and watering it with her tears.

What had she done?
Coming to this lonesome place
All alone with her desires—her desires that were not going anywhere.

She wanted men
She wanted their white seeds inside her, she wanted them spilling into her like night stars.

Now she had nothing to talk to but the birds who showed her the ways of the watering holes and where the berries were. She'd take a handful of fruits, dry them out on rocks, then place a few in the hood of her cloak.

The rest she left for the other animals

Before wandering on
On and on
And on and on
And on

In the dawns, she'd flip the rocks that proffered beads of dew. She'd suck the soft fur on her arms. It caught the damp like spiderwebs.

She sucked on her arms plenty.

She ate the desert dates
Soapberries
Balsam
Pearl plants
The seeds of butm trees she ground for oil

She'd slip her finger across the greased rock afterwards
She'd rub her lips
It was too much—
It was all too much

She wanted fresh wine and bodies

The bawdy tunes they used to sing together in the city streets
God
But God it had been good

Then
Terror
Those flashbacks to the boat,
She'd forced those poor sailors into every depravity.
She'd overpowered them with her will.

She was right to come here
To protect others from herself.

It took forty-seven years with her cheek and ears pressed up against the sand
For Mary of Egypt to hear the grains breathing back.
Each grain of sand breathing in and out was a body, she realised, a vessel.

After forty-seven years alone

She knew there were bodies all around her
They were breathing all over her
In the blue nights she heard all their breaths, all their breaths, coming together.

She never had been alone. She knew that now.

Across the centuries, monks from the desert were travelling up the coasts of North Africa and Europe. They were sailing from Scetes and past Cádiz. They were settling in various places. Eventually they formed small monasteries in Gaul, Lérins, Tours, Auxerre. Their distinct form of Christianity travelled with them. Now the people in those villages were being asked to love one's neighbour *without malice, without jealousy, without fear, without terror*—for that was a Great Commandment; the love of one's neighbour was up there with the greatest of all.

In the fifth century Amma Sarah's words travelled to the green-grey islands at Europe's western edge—they arrived in Ireland; they travelled to Iona, to many small islands largely beyond the sphere of Roman influence. What did those words say?

'If I prayed to God that all people should approve of my conduct, I should find myself a penitent at the door of each one. Instead I'll pray that my heart may be pure toward all.'

The land on the western edge became a burning bush entwined with pagan visions. New chants began to ring out as the people kindled their fires, as they milked their cows and spun their wool and made their shoes.

Chants that referenced a love of peace and thunder
Water-dogs and kestrel hawks
Wrens and limpets
And every raspberry
Sleeping bird
And dark marsh alder

The whole island was drawn into those verses

And the new Christian God, in those rural backwaters influenced by desert-drifting saints, was not a bearded man living in golden clouds, looking down. That is perhaps a Roman version of God derived from images of the sky-god Jupiter.
This new God was formless, genderless, infinite.

I always see a white beard when I hear the word *God*, so I've been reshaping the kindling words so I can bring my contemporary heart out to meet them. When I go past my mean neighbour's house, I silently chant to myself,

Kindle within my heart
A flame of love to my neighbour,
To my foe, to my friend, to my kindred all,
To the brave, to the knave, to the thrall.

Sometimes I get the words wrong, and maybe I am offending by not using the word *God*. But I want to sincerely make my way into the past, when love was the gold bending bodies to the moon, when love was the gold flowing through time's pattern.

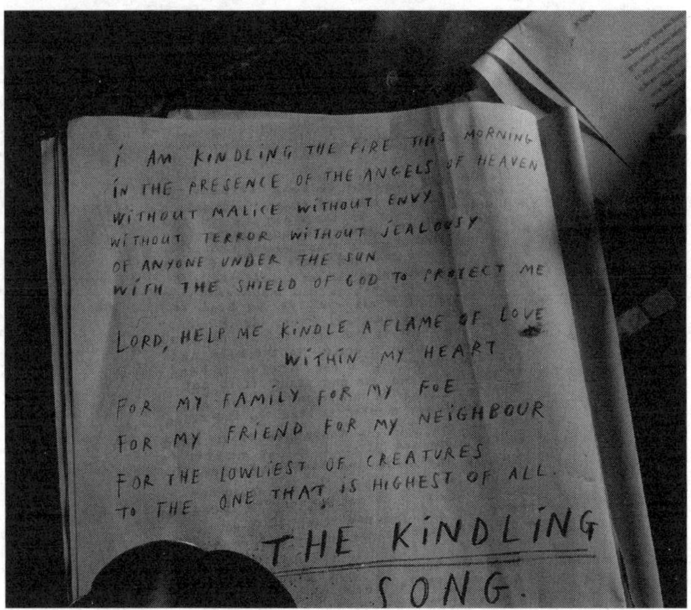

Saying the old words before bed, the moments between waking and sleeping have been filling up with images both fresh and ancient, with the sanctity of sleeping birds—with the ptarmigan in her mountain nest, with the heron fading in the pointed trees. It feels good. I think it's the old lullabies I've been needing.

Mary Macleod lived alone on Barra. She was old and poor, and in the nineteenth century she told Alexander Carmichael as he travelled the islands, setting down desert words for the *Carmina Gadelica*,

'In the time of my father and my mother there was no man in Barra who would not take off his bonnet to the white sun of power, nor a woman in Barra who would not bend her body to the white moon of the seasons. No, my dear, not a man nor a woman in Barra. And old people will still be doing this, and I will be doing it myself sometimes. Children mock me, but if they do, what of that? Is it not much meeter for me to bend my body to the sun and to the moon and to the stars than to the son and daughter of Earth like myself?'

This week, I've been writing down the same line again and again.

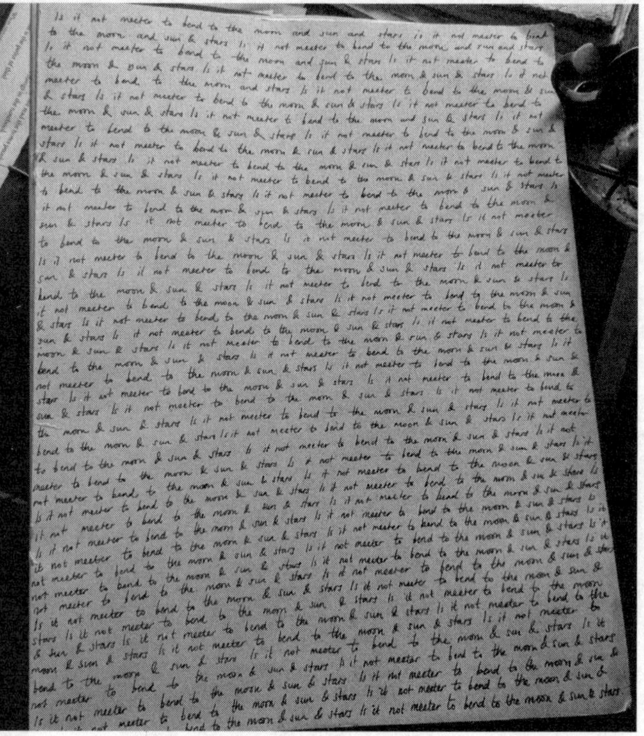

May 29

This week I've been reading a science paper from Cornell that says while deserts may seem like lifeless and inert places, sand dunes not only grow and move and interact with each other, the grains of sand are porous, inhaling and exhaling tiny amounts of water vapour. 'The wind flows over the dune and as a result creates imbalances in the local pressure, which literally forces air to go into the sand and out of the sand. So, the sand is breathing, like an organism breathes,' the lead author Michel Louge writes.

Summer

Mosquito

June 1

On Friday I did my kitten work. I watched the Chinese documentary *Amongst White Clouds*. Near the end of the film, a Chán hermit hooked a plastic pipe from a mountain spring far above her tiny hut, so she'd have fresh water flowing towards her kitchen. While she was arranging the pipe, she said *this life it's hard, it's hard*. Yet she was laughing. She was laughing so much.

Watching her made me think of Yeo Yeo—a nun who lives in a temple on a busy street in Seoul. I was on an overnight stay at the monastery with a scattering of American theology students when I met her.

Yeo Yeo sat us down in the prayer hall and told us stories. She said she loved her Gillette Mach3. 'Know why?' she asked, bowing forward so we could see her shining skull. She said before she had a good razor, she used to get cuts while shaving her head as a beginner nun. 'This made summers meditating outside agony. The mosquitoes bit at every wound. They only came for me, not the other nuns and monks. For a long time I couldn't figure out why. Then I realised I'd been killing the mosquitoes' brothers and sisters each night in my room. I felt so bad! I went and apologised to them. For hours and hours I bowed to the mosquitoes. I said, "Thank you, you never killed me. Thank you!" I was never bitten by a mosquito again.'

Life could be horrible, was that what Yeo Yeo had been saying? But if you stopped fretting, the annoying diversions of life might flow over you?

Wasn't Yeo Yeo also saying that she avoided leafy paths in autumn, when there'd be a lot of insects hiding beneath the leaves? She performed a hundred and eight prostrations a day for them and all the other creatures she may have inadvertently harmed.

She was saying sorry and thank you and sorry and thank you constantly. I've decided that I'll love mosquitoes too. The first have just hatched in the puddles on the path.

To make suffering joy, I'll think from the insects' perspective when they're drinking my blood. The taste of my blood does make them giddy; it sends the neurons in a mosquito's second tongue absolutely sparkling. I can be giddy too. Then, when my arm gets itchy, I'm not going to scratch. I'm not going to do anything that comes naturally. What has acting naturally ever done for me?

I'll love the mosquitoes as Yeo Yeo does.

I've been waiting for winged things to drift by the train tracks.

The first mosquito, here she comes.

In my breath she senses a sweet river of carbon dioxide. This river is in all the animals she drinks from.

In the robins,
In the frogs,
In the cats,

In the horses,
In the snakes,
In the salamanders,
In the dogs.

I also have a slightly different aromatic note from other animals. On my skin and in my breath she senses the presence of octenol, mushroom alcohol. It's in us, corked wine, and morels.

She glides her mouthpiece in.
Her abdomen tilts up as she probes, then delves.

I can't feel her entering me.
She does it so slowly.

Now she's drinking, her transparent body is filling up; a ruby is swelling inside her as she experiences long seconds of pleasure.

If I had gold paint, I could dab her body while she drinks. If the weather stayed dry so the gold did not run off, in a few days I'd find her again. I'd squeeze her abdomen with the gentlest touch and feel a hard seed—the beginnings of a hundred eggs formed with the protein in my blood. There'll be larvae. Then pupae tumbling around in puddles and tin cans.

Her babies are going to look just like her. But a part of me will have formed them too.

Many of those mosquitoes will feed the animals that string the world with song. They'll feed the blue swallows and brown warblers. And young dragonflies. And gathering fish, and slinking salamanders, and skittering bats, and many spiders. Many, many spiders. Then the birds will eat the spiders, and the coyotes will eat the birds. And then maybe one day a coyote will eat me. I can feel small suns landing on my shoulders just thinking about it.

Mosquitoes droning in the air—two sound artists once tried to love it. A decade ago, Robin Meier and Ali Momeni created an installation using tiny microphones to amplify the noise made by mosquito wings.

In various galleries, Meier and Momeni played three male mosquitoes an artificial stimulus sound—in this case, a recording of drone-like traditional Indian Dhrupad singing. When the males they'd gently attached to a wire with beeswax heard this noise, they acted as if aroused by a female. They matched their wing beats to the sound while a gallery audience listened via loudspeakers.

Visitors were invited to quietly interact by offering a fingertip for a mosquito to lie on. They were asked to excite the mosquitoes with their breath. The work of art was described as a love song. It was named *Truce: Strategies for Post-Apocalyptic Computation.*

Now the sun is sliding across the mountains, it's sliding down the trees, and in this light these mosquitoes flying over the path are spun from gold. This one placing her mouthpiece into the fibres of my dress, she has wings like stained glass.

I'm sorry for blooming your ancestors' bodies into flowers, I tell her. *I'm sorry for turning the caravan walls red.*

Sitting on the concrete outside the flat, I begin counting my new bites by the door. He comes out and places a thumb in the inner corner of my eye. He tells me I'm bleeding. So I have eighteen bites at least. Each insect that drank my blood now has the energy to lay around a hundred eggs. I've helped make so many babies and it's only 9:00 am.

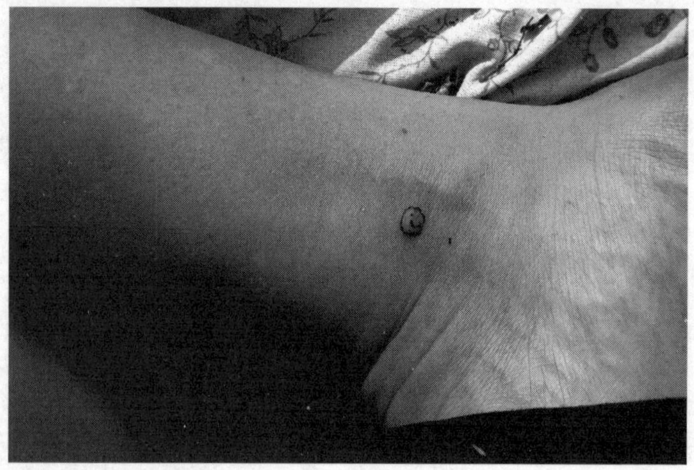

June 5

Inga reminded me that given how I keep talking about wanting a kaleyard, I'm probably in need of iron. I'm probably anaemic and the mosquitoes likely weren't going to make a hundred eggs each with my blood.

Even helping one or two eggs along is so much.

June 6

Tonight in the bath I read a Welsh epigram from around the seventeenth century.

'I thought, if only I could marry I should have nothing but song and dancing; what did I have, though, after marriage, but to rock the cradle and hush the baby?'

Being with the mosquitoes felt like dancing to me. I think I want to rock my way towards more of those moments.

Rats

June 7

I really think loving mosquitoes has been my best idea. Maybe I can love everything.

Instead of doing a kitten story today, I wrote about how, when scientists stroked and tickled rats' soft bodies and recorded the sounds they made with ultrasonic instruments, they'd hear giggling.

How I wish there were fields here. I wish there were rats!

Gnat

June 9

This morning I went to a free yoga class taught by a Chilean man. All the attendees were lying down in the basement gym before the class began. He said, 'All of you sit up! I'm telling a story!' He pulled a twig out from his bees' nest of hair and said, 'One day a little musk deer was grazing in the meadow when she noticed a scent more lovely than rose petals. It was, without a doubt, the loveliest scent in the world. The little musk deer was driven wild by that scent. Where did it come from? She searched among the rocks and flowers. She searched along the riverbanks. She got so frustrated, searching. For she could smell the scent everywhere, but she could not discover its source. Well, the little musk deer was a determined little musk deer. She decided that she'd never stop searching for that beautiful scent. She searched the entire valley. She went deep into the dark forests beyond and searched there. She travelled up high mountains and across the deserts. Searching for the scent, the little musk deer grew so frustrated with herself—and very weary. She died without realising the scent was right there, in her navel, all along.'

This week I've been watching two cinnamon deer. I've been choosing my outfits for visiting based on the advice given in a hunting forum. Now I know to wear a dress that's about the same green as the leaves. I've also been wearing a woven, red and white wool belt to break up my outline.

These two are mule deer. And though their bodies are sweetened with scent glands, they do not produce musk. This is lucky for them, because if they did their great-great-grandparents would likely have been turned into perfume.

To get up close to a deer, you're supposed to walk quietly like a weasel. I've never tried to walk like a weasel before, but it feels natural to go stealing through green growth while placing one foot down as gently as possible—the outside of the ball first, then the inside, the toes, then ever so quietly, the heel. On and on like a weasel I go.

In truth I don't need to walk like a weasel. These two male deer who live by the town portion of the creek, they're utterly habituated.

It's nice to be here in the grass, drawing them. They're so close I could reach out and play their ribs with a fingertip. I could rest a book between their antlers like Saint Kenneth. I'd read the pages while we walked together through the forest.

Lying about in the warm grasses, drawing one deer as he turns his neck and sucks his tail into the shape of a pencil, it's nice to make one continuous line without looking down. Sometimes the drawing falls off the page and onto the grass.

Oh. Now I'm looking down at the grass, I'm realising for a gnat there's no difference between a pen and a spear.

June 10

This week I performed a hundred and eight prostrations for a gnat whose life was quite short.

Grove

June 11

I've been pulling the ends of raw dough into wayward snakes all evening. It's horrible tearing mushroom clouds off the master dough, seeing skin coming off in sheets and bodies evaporating in flames. All that money burning, and orchids and cats and trees and trams and children's lunchboxes and two hundred thousand cheeks while Truman and Churchill applauded the success of Little Boy and Fat Man from a distance. Terrible, gripping the kitchen counter then bursting into forgetful action on hearing the oven timer. Putting on the oven gloves, opening the door, tilting away from the heat, placing the pulled raw dough on the stone, closing the door, taking off the gloves. Lying on the carpet. Remembering. Tapping a pencil. Writing a message to the mayor asking him to become a Mayor for Peace. Touching a twig. Playing with a ball. Hearing the timer. Opening the oven. Tapping at bread bottoms. Switching off the oven. Putting on my raincoat and doing up the buttons. Picking up the IKEA bag with the camping mat, the hat, and the tea flask already stashed; putting on the brown boots and going out the door—one baguette stashed between my jacket and jumper. Three gold slashes against my arm and my head's full of small dogs and gobstoppers while the rain pours like silver milk and everything outside's fizzing. Walking through the streets and into the woods. Moths flinging themselves up around my ankles and there's a man stopped on top of the hill—for him I silently chant *a flame of love to my foe, to my friend, to my kindred all* till he's moving and I'm turning off the path and making my way to the old deer bed by the water. Trees holding the sottobosco darkness of the old paintings. The rain getting softer. The world getting so soft, sounds so soft as water goes falling from leaf to leaf to ground. Small plants rising through rain sequins. Rain rotating mosquitoes round and round. Spreading out my camping mat. Placing the IKEA bag over my legs. My coat coming off. My jumper coming off. And then my vest. No need for fig leaves or razors. Warm rain's touching the animal skin on my chest—warm rain's touching this body that's swelling into earth.

The next afternoon, it was still raining still. I went up the hill, to the notebook I'd left on the bench.

People write in it most days.

A small child named Luka must have recently dropped a berry from his mouth upon the central pages—now there are seeds and juice where he drew his portrait. He must have been excited, drawing above the town with one strawberry tucked inside his cheek. Drawing waving hands and a mouth is exciting at any age. It was exciting seeing his mother writing L U K A. As he opened his mouth to let in an O of air, one small wet berry fell.

Luka has been here. And on the next page here are the marks of Inga. She has thanked The Boys for the beer they left on the hill for a stranger.

These people are people of the woods. They write of the trees.

Someone has written 'a bee landed on my yellow dress; we were both looking for flowers'.

Someone has written a series of Mary Oliver poems.

People are always leaving Mary Oliver poems.

People are writing about their emotions. Those are the notes I notice. Those are the feelings I cannot talk about to strangers or kin. And so this notebook reads like great literature to me. Yet these people writing are not Tolstoy. They touch the same pears in the grocery store as I do. We encounter the same skies. And sometimes we set our thoughts down, in this small notebook on the hill above the town.

One person has signed their note 'Anonymous'. They've written that they've been struggling with their drug addiction again. They've been so afraid of disappointing their family and friends.

The next person has replied to Anonymous that they're not as anonymous as they think.

They've written, 'I'm here for you, whenever you need. I love you. You-know-who.'

Someone has copied a quote from Federico García Lorca.

Someone has written,

'I saw my first rufous hummingbird along this trail a few days ago; the night that it snowed. Did you know they make a buzzing noise? I realised I may have one nesting in my garden; I often hear the unmistakable buzzing and once saw one hovering above me while I pulled weeds. I think this is my new favourite bird. The evening I saw my first hummingbird was the same night I first spotted her blonde hair

against her green jacket, walking deeper into the woods as the rain fell. I feel as if I've been mesmerised by the small moment we shared as she looked over her shoulder one last time, although I'm not sure if she even noticed me. Perhaps I'm entranced by the idea that, like the hummingbird, she could become someone special to me. Perhaps we could find a quiet spot in the forest to watch birds, or find new places to explore together. Or maybe I'm just projecting. I will try not to think of you when the hummingbird comes to visit.'

I've been walking up and down the rainy hills, wondering how to reply.

Up and down the path, I've been thinking of what to write.

While walking today, I saw a deer place his tongue round a stalk of white cherry flowers. Petals flowed over his forehead and landed on his back as fawn spots. Perhaps I should write about him—the freshness of youth.

I saw a little girl sobbing among the trees. Her mother said she was sad because she couldn't take the woods home with her. Perhaps I should write about youth's sweet greed.

July 19

New notes have been joining the old ones while I have been walking up and down the hill:

'Pebbles was here'

'Robi saw a cat!'

How many sentences there are in the world to love. How much we are trying to reach each other in every possible way.

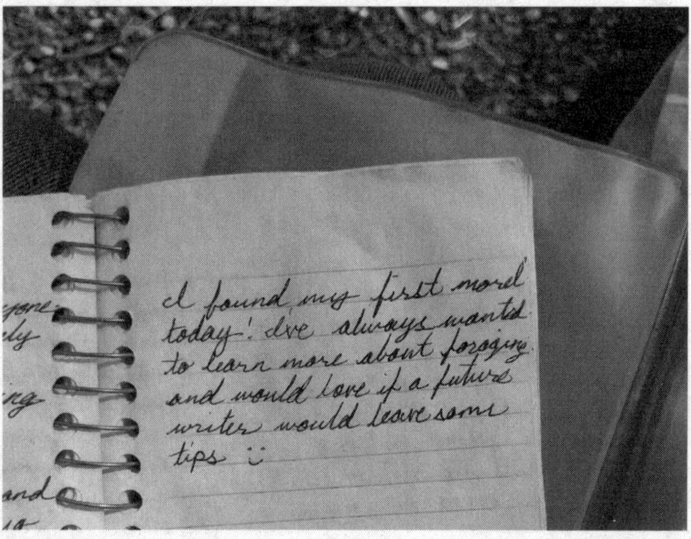

Today I wrote back, 'Just after you saw me disappear into the bushes, my mind began moving with the grasses.

'That peaceful feeling. I didn't know it was still possible. I used to feel it as a child. The trees and sky touched my interior. They floated through my ribs and often stayed there. Lying down in the grasses, I'd feel the daisies weaving between my fingers. They made me wonder about meanings. I'd wonder why a hedge was called a hedge and not a himminy and not an egg. I'd wonder why an egg was not called a peg.

'The feeling of childhood—of the world moving both inside and outside me—faded for a long time. It's fading again, yet I hope to hold on to some of its sensation for a few days longer. For the leaves now feel very soft.

'I liked reading about your experience with the hummingbirds. Perhaps now you have a quiet space for yourself in your garden, they know you're serious about wanting to meet them.

'A robin has been singing while I've been writing to you. Down in the town, I can hear the bulldozers. The rocks, now released from the immense pressure of the earth's surface, are cracking like eggs in the night.

'If the rocks talk, they must speak very slowly. Given their age, their speech must be beautifully languid. For the old speak slowly and carefully. And the young speak quickly and carelessly. So one sentence from a rock must be so slow. Slower than our life spans. Perhaps this is why we can never know what they're saying?

'I lived in Korea for a year. I often felt overwhelmed by sensory input there. I would go to the temples or mountains to find quiet. One Saturday I went to White Tiger Mountain. I hiked up the snowy path and encountered few people between the pine trees. Near the top I saw a Shinto woman chanting and clapping tin pans before a large rock. She was making offerings of noodles and rice wine while two fat cats scrambled around her like mountain goats. Before then, I'd never imagined there being rocks with spirits in them. Now I think there might be spirits in them.

'All this to say, I'm glad of the things you wrote.

'I've been trying to listen to the birds more, since seeing your note.

'The last time I heard a hummingbird, I was walking here with a stranger. The hummingbird was red and shining just above our heads. My arm involuntarily reached towards its body.

'I don't know why I try to touch birds.

'I suppose not far down the line, all sorts of calamities were happening to them in hands like mine. My hands and heart are the result of others who could catch and kill a stormy petrel then run a thread through its body, turning it into a candle.

'There are generations of people in me who were eating puffin porridge. Maybe there is a memory of such a meal in my hands—and that is why I am always trying to touch the birds? There are memories of bird oil sitting in neat jarred rows in darkened cupboards, of the beaks of solan geese holding down thatch.

'The place I like best in the world is dangerous. My father says that, a century ago, a drunken farmer lost a bet in a local pub; he got on his horse still bleezing and rode all along the terrifying sea cliffs and cauldrons; the next morning he woke up and realised with a fright what he'd done—he had a heart attack and died right there and then.

'I go to those same cliffs, but not by pony. I just crawl along the skinny promontories till I'm at the burrows. In my shadows the birds see my forebears who dashed along high strips of rock like this. It takes time for them to relax amid my presence. Then clouds of rainbow beaks emerge. They look at me while I eat Hobnobs.

'If we have souls, are they in the birds? In the pigeons and the crows? Is that why it feels right when we make a quiet space for them? How much the birds like us to be quiet. It is as if they are curious about us too. It is as if they do want to see us.

'Last time I was with a stranger in these woods, I asked him if we find birds beautiful because from an evolutionary standpoint we want to eat them. I felt a real tension in him as he pointed at the valley below us. "See that valley?" he said. "If that valley is the human mind, then what we understand, what scientists understand, is the size of a leaf. Puffins are beautiful," he said. "That's all."

'Hummingbirds have no knees.

'I wish you well on walking like one.'

Fire

June 21

I know a little of what Orcadians did for the winter solstice—they'd make little golden cakes out of bere barley to symbolise the sun. I know more of what they did for the summer solstice. Great-Uncle wrote that they got rowdy with great fires. Night of Johnsmas and everyone in the parish was carrying baskets filled to the brim with old oars and tables and smashed-up cribs to the top of the highest hill. They stacked odds and ends ever higher into a pyre.

The whole village eventually gathered in the dusk. Meat and fish and homebrew simmered. Quiet descended as a crone placed the bone of a cow in the unlit heart of the bonfire, followed by a fistful of butter.

An elder brought a torch to wood. The people shouted as lights emerged. Scents of burning fat and hay arose as flames sparked into blue hands. Flames caught the clouds. The people chugged brew till they were cradling the moon in their arms; till they were stamping their feet with the flames.

It's summer solstice night, and I've gone to the lake with Inga and my husband. This silver desert has turned green again. It's been raining for weeks now and the avenues of birches are lighting up like gas lamps.

As soon as I looked at him look at Inga looking at the digger parked near a pile of driftwood, I knew what would happen.

By nightfall, she was sitting on top of the pyre. He was bringing a flaming lichen over. A small stream of smoke. Sounds of twigs catching alight. Then a bloom of heat. White logs bursting. Then Inga was scrabbling down laughing, her bright hair swinging. Flames caught flames until the sky was opaque with firelight, until the stars were all blotted out and I was stepping forward, stepping back, making stars appear, then disappear, stepping forward, stepping back, I was running round suddenly afraid asking *are we safe, are we safe are we*, I was crouching down beside him and whispering *are we*—he was pulling me between his knees and making a hole in the earth with his index finger; he was taking my hand in his and bringing our clasped palms down into the soaked clay, *we're safe*.

We were safe, and on the tips of the wild grasses, dew drops were reflecting the fire in thousands. I reached out to touch a stalk. Water beads were falling down my wrists. Fire-dew for us all. Fire-dew on my ears, on his brows, on her elbow.

I woke to white embers and Inga beaming. She led me to a hollowed-out tree on the edge of the forest-shore. Tilting our heads into its dusky void, our ears made pictures of shingling seashells.

You're really moving to the ocean now, I said to Inga. She touched my shin with her foot and said *you're going to the ocean soon too*.

Creek

June 28

The weather changed in an instant. 17 36 37 37 38. Now parts of the forest across the border have set on fire. Smoke's drifting in from the next province over. The sky's the brown of stockings and the sun has turned into a distant pink ball and smoke's curling through our room and slipping under the door. It's crawling into the crows while they stand on branches with their red mouths gaping. And the fish are floating dead on the hot lakes and last night I saw a group of men glowing pale as candles in the water while smoke drifted in around them. They were standing half-submerged and gasping in a small circle. One man dipped his body into the water and rose back up. His abs were glistening as he ran his hands through his hair. *I feel so alive*, he said.

I feel like death, his friend replied.

June 29

Sky's the brown of soup and I feel like death.

Smoke

July 9

Brown skies driving to the airport. Mosquitoes trailing us like bridesmaids as we stand by YEG's sliding doors; he opens my right hand and places a bone in my palm. Says it's an elk toe. He's plaited three green threads and run them through the bone's hollow. *You did this?* He's nodding and leaning towards my right ear, saying *elk toes have been found sewn on ancient clothing—the clothes people went raving in*. He's closing my fingers around the toe. He's closing his hand around mine. *All those people waving and arcing, all those bones rattling, can you hear them?*

Yes, I say, nodding his stubble against my ear.

Then he's turning to open the passenger door and he's lifting the puppy from the seat so her tail's swishing against our foreheads; he's bringing her down between our chests so our three breaths are coming together, and I don't know what I'm doing as I enter the airport's revolving doors alone and there's only my own breath.

He made my wedding ring from bone. He carved it from a piece of moose antler he'd found in a garage. I wore it in the bath and in the shower. I wore it while riding an escalator. I wore it and chewed it constantly, and then it snapped.

Wedding

July 14

The fields as seen from the train window were soft and denuded; the women were glamorous. In my carriage, they wore gold hoops and centre partings; they looked like queens in their white trainers, with their silk skirts flowing like rivers. I felt my naked ears and the elk bone strung around my neck and I felt like a bumpkin beside them. It was the lifestyle section of the newspaper left behind on the train table that did it. The headlines in *T2* were asking if I wanted that natural, glowing look and the best of the season's denim dresses. I did. I did I did. At the same time I knew this was the last thing I wanted. I took out my pen and began writing one blue-black word on top of the printed sentences. The word that means to rotate, to spin celestial—I wrote it over and over again. But it wasn't my word. It wasn't the right word. Not from me. Across the travel section the food section the wine reviews the beauty pages I wrote out the old word. The word as old as revolution. *Gaol*. Pronounced 'gill'. It's the only Gaelic I know. Soon I'll learn more.

After Edinburgh, the fields and coastline became rougher and darker. A year since I'd last been home, the world so rough and dark. Now standing at the terminus was my mother.

Her hair now fully silver.

Silvers in mine now too.

She's wrestling my rucksack from me. She's whispering in my ear. She's flinging me to my knees with laughter, this laughter she's been gifting me with all my life.

'Let's get you home,' she says. 'He'll be asleep, but he's doing well.'

She says it again, like a surprise. 'He's really doing well.'

In the morning I lay in bed late. I dreamed of the farm girls who'd slept in this room before me—the fishwives who'd come inland to barter with them. Fishwives who loved silver coins and black cats and itchy feet and a loose eyelash upon the cheek, for it all meant the men might be coming back. When they reached this house, they slipped haddocks into mucky hands—they accepted eggs and cheese in return. The dust and salt of those girls is mixed in this room with mine.

I went downstairs and found him in the kitchen. He was drawing imaginary maps on scraps of paper. He said a badger had burrowed into the garden early that morning. The badger sent bees bursting from their underground hive. He'd watched amazed as bees clung to the badger's pelt, as soil spurted up in thick black fountains beneath the badger's talons. The bees were trying to sting him, but the badger's fur was too thick for their defence to work; he just sat down peacefully and sucked babies from his paws while plated with furious golden armour. My dad looked like the sun shining through paper as he spoke of them.

'Shall we go out to see the flowers?' he said. We went out in our pyjamas. There was a cool dampness in the air that I'd forgotten about. There was so much I'd forgotten about as he showed me the wood sage the milk thistle the baldmoney the bronze fennel the betony. I wrote the names of the flowers down, the names were so good. Then finally we reached the lamb's lugs. Lamb's lugs soft and furry and pale green.

We bent down and touched the leaves.
He gently picked two of them, then held them to his ears.

'You are like a child,' I said, reaching over to take one.

'You are my child,' he said, smiling.

'Are the plants your children?'

'They're God's children,' he replied, nodding.

We sat under the beech tree and watched the meggie-mony-feet.

'Why are you patting your feet against the ground?' I asked.

'I'm excited to be seeing you. I'm excited about the gulls. Soon enough, herring gulls will come flocking to the fresh-turned soil out there,' he said, looking out at the fields. 'They'll pat their feet against the morning earth and the worms do feel those vibrations. Every instinct in their body tells them a predatory mole is burrowing horizontally towards them. Sensing those tremors, the worm begins to move. She squeezes her body up, quick as she can, up through the soil. She breaks desperately through the rich black surface and into the light. Morning uncoils on her back. Her five hearts open wide. And whose glaucous eyes are watching that soft blind body?'

'No!'

'Down a gull's gullet she goes.'

'That stupid worm,' I said. 'Why did she not just stay where she was?'

'No point blaming the worm, baba,' he replied. 'Though it was she who moved her body upwards—what's to be done? She was only following her reflexes. Her end is akin to fate. It wasn't a choice. Anyway, by thresher or by old age, she will inevitably die. The gull will give her a quick death. Better that than her meeting the mole. A mole will stretch her body till it's free of soil—then he might very well bite her head off. She'll be alive, headless and alive, and he'll store her in his underground kitchen chamber with hundreds of other living worms. All of them wriggling about ceaselessly down there. Imagine that, baba. That's a terrible sort of half-life.'

I patted the lawn and thought of the worms. I played with the grass. I patted my dad's arm and said I had work to do. He nodded and looked down at his knees.

July 17

This evening was my childhood friend Mhairi's wedding. Outside there was grass and fountains. The sky was fading golden. In the marquee, silver balloons were drifting up to the ceiling. We were getting a little drunk, seated beside each other, Evan and I. Close friends since we were ten, I was asking if he'd ever move back from Moscow. He shook his head and said why would he move back here? 'In Russia one isn't expected to talk on and on about the weather and the new meal deal at Marks & Spencer. On walking home after a party there, I'm often overcome by a mix of elation and gratitude, I'm on the verge of tears because of the conversations I've had. In Russia there's no shame in feeling sorrow, and so it's possible to talk truthfully of one's emotions. It's not possible to talk deeply here. If I reveal how I am feeling, I'll receive sympathy and little clucks of pity. But sympathy is not empathy. Empathy is a shared feeling—a bridge that connects us. Sympathy is something else—it's when someone looks down from their high tower and coos *oh poor you.* Yet why look down on another's sorrows? Sorrow is universal. It's hiding from such emotions that hurts deeply—yet the culture here is dedicated to doing just that. The questions I get. *Oh isn't it cold where you are? Isn't it corrupt? Oh don't you miss home? And aren't the people poor? And why don't they smile? And why aren't they friendly? And I wouldn't like the weather there. And that horrible little man in charge!* The glee you know they feel as they concoct this terrible Russia in their minds. How much they want you to be cold! How much they want the Russian people to be unfriendly! It makes them feel fortunate by comparison. This British idea of happiness—this thinking that if we can just get all our ducks lined up in a row, if we can just have a house and a pension we'll be safe from all ills—that's such a false dream. Dostoevsky was highly sceptical of the idea that happiness could be achieved through the evasion of suffering by pursuing comfort. He thought it impossible to achieve joy in this way—for we will always find a reason to suffer. Better to accept one's discomforts and look for happiness therein.' Evan picked up his phone and began to scroll. 'Here it is,' he said. 'If you regard suffering and pain as evil, as detestable, as deserving of annihilation, well then beside your religion of pity you have yet another religion in your heart, and this is perhaps the mother of the religion of pity—the religion of smug ease. Ah, how little you know of the happiness of man, you comfortable ones! For happiness and misfortune are brother and sister who grow tall together, or, as with you, remain small together.'

I said he didn't need to read out quotes to me. I said I dreamed of material comforts and my dream home all the time. I vividly saw its windows and trees, its stone walls and rafters; I'd be scrumming potash into flagstones and watching chimney swallows forming cups from mud, my niece and nephews would be coming over on Sundays, I'd be pulling off their bright wellies, I'd be on my knees and—'

'That's such a stupid dream,' Evan said, accepting the golden en croûte dish the waiters were bringing round. 'You get bored within two minutes of being home. Anyway, suffering always pursues us. Even in your so-called dream house, you'll suffer from whatever brought you towards dreaming of that habitation in the first place.'

'It's not stupid. It's stupid that it costs a lot of money now to share a roof with a sheep, a rat, and a plough. It's stupid that the coastline's rising and there'll soon be fishes darting up the chimney spouts. Anyway we all have romantic dreams. You can't say you don't. You moved to Russia because of literature. Maybe you're still projecting a kind of high-minded beauty onto your encounters there. Yet those novels that brought you there are from another time, and the Russians you know are living today. So are they really talking like Anna Karenina? Are we not all living as new people in a different era? Your friends are wealthy and urban, so they are as immersed in technology as anyone. My husband, when I first moved to Canada, was doing his thesis on nature and technology. These terms mean different things to different people.'

'I know what you mean by them.'

'So for his thesis he spent three weeks immersed in technology. He was talking to chatbots while showering, he was creating sound pieces in the early hours by recording household noises. From his perspective, the experiment was going well. On many days, his immersion in technology was nearly perfect, with only a few minutes spent awake or asleep without some kind of digital input. He noticed that in his "technologically" extended body, his actual physical body felt few sensations. He never felt the wind in his hair or the sun on his skin. He never got too hot or too cold. Emotionally, he began to feel flat and disconnected too. His physical life took on a sort of imaginary quality while his digital life began to feel more real. He began to have trouble dealing with the other people around him—in fact he felt better alone. After those three weeks, he temporarily lost the desire to go outside, or be with people, or eat healthy foods, or be still and quiet. The day after his experiment was over, he went hiking with me, out of a sense of duty rather than desire. He found his muscles had degraded. The next day even his bones hurt. He had never had that experience before. He checked the scale to discover he had gained about ten pounds. When balanced against lost muscle mass it felt like a drastic change.

'In the following days he suffered several anxiety attacks—the first he'd had. These might have had many causes, but he felt the most significant was the transition from his immersed state to reality. Somehow, his mind could no longer organise itself to deal with problems rationally. His feelings could not be compartmentalised. Instead they overwhelmed him. His heart would race and his body would be jittery until he found a piece of media to distract him again.'

'Where did he do this?' Evan asked, stuffing a forkful of peas in his mouth.

'In our flat. Then he went to some woods near his friends' commune. He tried to avoid using the most electric items while there. For example he used a firesteel instead of a lighter to build a fire for breakfast. He slept in a willow yurt instead of a tent. He wore woollen jumpers rather than fleeces, and read only books that had been written before the Industrial Revolution.

'Near the end of his second week in the woods, he had planned to visit a local farmer whose cow his friends owned a share in.

This share entitled them to a gallon of milk, and since they were away, they had given the milk share to him. He walked down the hill and was immediately surrounded by four large barking dogs. After five minutes, most of the dogs had lost interest in snarling, and he was able to move on unharassed, if a little shaken. He cut through the woods and grabbed a large stick, thinking it a basic maxim of wilderness survival that it's better to have a big stick and not need it than to need a big stick and not have it. The wooded trail hit a main road, and he walked on. A few kilometres later six dogs careened out of a dilapidated trailer and surrounded him. Their jaws frothed and foamed as they circled him, barking violently. He imagined himself lying in the road as the dogs feasted on his entrails. After a tense few minutes of brandishing his stick at their feinting attacks, a croaking voice from the trailer shouted at the dogs and they ran back to their home. This second dog attack was much more frightening.

'He walked on and found the farm. He entered the building he had been told held the milk. He found the fridge where the milk was and put the gallon in his bag. He saw the farmer outside and asked if he could have some potatoes. The farmer said he could, but only if he bought fifty pounds, which was too heavy an amount to carry home. Then the farmer declared that while he was thinking about it, he couldn't have the milk because the cow was short on milk and he wanted the milk for himself. He told him he had informed his friends by mobile phone that there was no milk this week.

'My husband tried to tell him about his experiment and why he was so hungry, but the words wouldn't come. He was having too hard a time keeping his emotions in check. He took the milk from his bag, handed it to the farmer and left glassy-eyed. Outside he contemplated the dogs he would have to fight to get home, and he sat, and he wept. Hunger and anxiety began to manifest themselves as real parts of the natural world. He began to have a better appreciation for foresight, planning, and restraint.

'One afternoon he asked one of the land residents if she might spare some food. She said she wouldn't spare anything she had grown, it was precious to her, but that he was welcome to come to dinner.

'Cleaned up, he went for dinner, and had his first real conversation in two weeks. He may as well have been eating at a banquet table with all the greatest and kindest people to have ever lived. It was the essence of kindness and warmth. Knowing he was trying to live without technology, they even lit candles for him instead of switching on the lights.

'On the last night of his experiment, he took his sleeping bag to a portion of land that was legislated by the co-op agreement to never have any human constructions on it. He climbed a steep mossy hill strewn with gigantic fallen cedar trunks. He had intended to arrive earlier, but because he had no watch, he did not know the time. He did not make it to his destination until it was very difficult to see. He scrabbled up the hill to a spot that looked big and flat enough to sit upon, just to discover that it wasn't. With darkness fast approaching, he threw some rocks down the hill to hollow out a sort of chair shape in the mossy hillside. He had about a foot of flat ground in front of him before a thirty-foot drop to the forest floor. He would be able to stand to pee, but attempting to move anywhere would be unwise. He sat there wrapped in his sleeping bag, and waited as darkness became complete. There, alone in the forest, he spent the night in vigil.

'It was a long twelve-hour night, being uncomfortable and precariously perched as he was, but still he dozed off in spite of his efforts to stay awake. At one point in the night, the constancy of the babbling brook was pierced by the shrieking call of a strange unidentified animal. It was a cry that shook any drowsiness from him. He shouted out a fearful response and the rest of the night was silent. When dawn broke, he climbed down from his perch. He did not come home with the power to bestow boons. However, he did feel less afraid of the darkness.

'After those three weeks, he would sit and look around at the many different trees and think about how they relate to one another. He would think about the many different people he has known in his life and his relationship to them. He wrote with a pen instead of typing. To do so, his mind had to slow down, form whole sentences, and wait while his hands carefully traced his ideas on the page. For quite a while, he was taking great pleasure in watching and feeling the words trace themselves on the page. As his mind moved more slowly, he felt like he was able to find greater clarity. His thoughts seemed to emerge better-formed and required less revision.

'During his time in nature, he experienced the full range of emotions—happiness, sadness, fear, anger, awe—he pondered those states, and felt as healthy and clear-minded as he ever had. In this period, I suppose I see him as a sort of Isaac Newton character, pulling up his stockings, then darkening his room in Cambridge till only a small hole remains in the shutter through which sunlight can enter. One beam of flat white light passes through the glass he's holding in his hand and then, on the far wall, a spectacular multicoloured band of light appears. A rainbow of emotion. A prism. To me, it sounds like he was experiencing something similar to your experiences at parties in Moscow? How is that? At a party in a city where everyone has smartphones? Your parties are nothing like embarking on a vigil in the forest at night, and yet—'

Evan cleaned his knife against the side of his plate and said perhaps societies that had long been culturally disinclined from hiding their emotions used phones differently, in a way that did not flatten the inner life.

'Are you sure about that?' I asked.

'I'm not sure,' he replied, 'but suffering is like breathing. There's no life without it.'

'I hate to see unhappiness in others,' I said, nodding to the waiter for more wine. 'Hearing my father pacing in the morning, I wish him an easier time of it.'

'Wishing your father this British idea of happiness—you're violating his soul.'

'I'm violating his soul!'

'His experiences of sickness hold meaning, even if they can't be seen.'

'This collective British idea of happiness you're talking of, it's probably only in the Victorian era that we started to collectively prize an emotional state that's equal parts stoic and infantile. Before then, away from the centres of power, the people were not suppressing their hearts—they were performing keening rituals during times of sadness; alongside every praise poem they had songs for people leaving that were full of sorrow and lamentations.

Stoicism was only forced on children once the boarding school system became fashionable among the upper classes.

'That system came in once all the mummies and daddies were going away to their new colonial posts in India and elsewhere.

'That repression of emotions foisted on homesick pupils in private schools filtered through the social classes as an ideal way of being.

'It must have filtered into me all these years later. Why have I been ignoring those old ways? All year I've been trying to become a Stoic, Evan. Why is that? What do the ancient Greeks have to do with me? Maybe what I should be doing is keening. If keening's in my heart.'

Evan finished his wine and said, 'If it feels more right to you, then sure.'

That night I danced with my own shadow and thought I would go back to my husband.

The next morning I took a long bath, then in the afternoon I walked with my mother along Fisher Walk.

We walked through tremendous low fields that had run green then brown then green then brown for centuries. We climbed over rocky walls and spiky wires. We walked until fields turned to marshes and oystercatchers flew overhead. I said I'd been emailing an artist whose last artwork involved singing like an oystercatcher. She wore red tights and stood on the shores of Canna with a vocal ensemble while singing a mimetic score to the seabirds—I'd seen videos of the performance on the internet. I'd written to her because I'd been reading ancient bird chants in the *Carmina Gadelica*.

When I wrote to Hanna, I said something like, 'Listening to you mimicking the water birds, I felt maybe I've been hearing something of that past, slipping into the present.'

She replied, 'To me mimesis is a form of empathy. It's an extension towards the more than human—towards all that's calling around us.'

Mum asked why I was suddenly interested in mimesis. I said I liked moments where humans and animals encountered one another. Had she not known that? I'd been away, she said, touching the small of my back. I said I loved stories of saints and beasts, of Saint Cuthbert and the otter. Saint Cuthbert walking down alone to the seashore after dark. Down beneath the night clouds he stood in the black sea. With the seventh-century waves lapping about his arms he recited the Psalms until dawn. And what was he saying but *laudate eum sol et luna laudate eum omnes stellae et lumen* praise ye him, sun and moon. He was thanking the moon, he was thanking the stars, he was saying alleluia for hours and hours. He was saying thank you until daybreak and when he finished his hymns and waded back onto the beach a pair of otters always came out of the water and rubbed his feet dry with their fur. They tenderly lapped his ankles with their rough little tongues until there was a union between them and I find that touching. Unions, I like those. The coming together of separate bodies. What we create from those moments could be so imaginative.

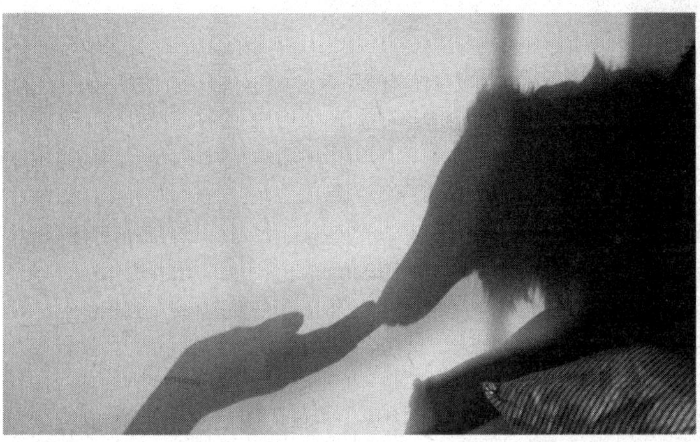

And while the story of Saint Cuthbert is likely a fable, Great-Granny was real. Her singing to the seals, the seals drifting in and singing back, that was possible. When seals were hipped animals wandering the shores, I suppose they had regular ears made for air, but as they spent more time in the water, their bodies adapted to exploring fields of fish—now a seal can follow the wakes of underwater animals with their sensitive whiskers, but they don't hear so well on the shore; their bodies are water-sleek and they've only tiny holes on the outsides of their heads to listen through, so what do they hear when they come up for air and a woman on the strand is calling out to them? Those sounds may enter their body in a way that's not so clear. The seals drift in closer. They listen, curious. And call back in a way that to our ears sounds so unbelievably haunting. Seals trying to commune with what lies immutably beyond them, that's real. Us trying to commune right there alongside them, that's real too.

Hoy

July 24

I set up the tent in the back garden so my books and pillows and I could live outside. Also I wanted a space where I could not feel the pressure of people so much loving me and willing happiness for me.

I wrote to Pluscarden Abbey, not far up the road, and asked if I could stay there for some nights. I'd only gone once. Copying the people around me, I'd knelt on a velvet cushion. The morning sun was streaming through huge, sakura-shaped windows above us. The light was flowing in golden tides across the inner stone walls; light was sweeping up the altar candles. It flowed up the monks' socks and sandals; it rendered the motes of dust visible. Joining in with the Gregorian chanting was the sounds of the doves in the trees outside. It felt like the roof had come off. It felt like vines and mice and birds were still teeming among the walls; the mice were. Before entering the chapel, I'd stood in the transept thumbing leaflets. On top of a blue booklet devoted to Saint Thérèse of Lisieux was one dark dropping like a grain of wild rice.

Pluscarden was a ruin for centuries. Plants and animals only lived among its stones till the end of the Second World War. Then five monks moved in. They slept on palliasses in the unglazed kitchen. They fixed the roofs.

They fixed the bell tower and each corner until, after twenty-six years of labour, the place was again recognised as a working abbey.

Pluscarden now is the only medieval monastery in Britain being used for its original purpose. Two dozen monks there go by the sixth-century Rule of Saint Benedict. They pray, and keep silent, and eat simple meals of bread, cheese, and honey. They do manual labour as stonemasons and beekeepers. One is a tailor who goes about making white woollen robes and black sashes for the others. Of their tasks, these monks say things like, 'We're not in a hurry. We have nothing better to do.'

'Sometimes the idea of having a wife can overwhelm one,' Father Benedict once told a visiting journalist. 'That's an ongoing battle till one dies. It's the same with things. It'd be quite nice if I could have a motorbike, or even an extra pair of socks. But for me, the joys outweigh the sorrows so much that the sorrows become irrelevant. Every single day, from the moment you get up to the moment you fall asleep, everything you are doing is completely worthwhile. There are moments when one is aware of really complete deep happiness. To lose the love of a wife to get the love of God more fully and directly, to be stripped of earthly goods in order to have the Kingdom, well what we get compared to what we give is ridiculously out of proportion.'

When I visited, most of the monks had been noticeably old—but one was around my age. When light streamed upon the back of his shaven head as he dished holy water into a bowl, a perfect rim of gold outlined his skull in the shape of a sickle. Watching that light, I felt all kinds of possibilities open up. For here was a man who did not know what OnlyFans was. This meant there were still chances of living outside the boundaries of this time. One might live according to sixth-century rules. One might live according to one's own rules.

Anyway, none of the monks replied to my email asking to stay. Perhaps I only imagined the existence of women's dorms.

Instead I took the ferry to Orkney.

On the ferry, I wondered what Isabelle Eberhardt would do. I went out and smoked cigarettes with some Shetlanders heading home to Lerwick. I got off the ferry around midnight and found my hostel.

In the morning, I put on my necklace and the red dress Inga had gifted me. I drank coffee at a café on Broad Street. My throat hurt. I shouldn't have tried to be like Isabelle.

I visited St. Magnus Cathedral, where old interior pillars stretched like rusty nails towards the vaulted ceiling. Footsteps were rising with them and falling back down as feathers. It was the Norsemen who built this place from red and gold sandstone a thousand years ago. They built it as a pilgrimage site in the midst of a busy sea road. They believed in a world of fourfold souls with *fylgjur* guiding us. Our bodies they saw as mere shells, while dwelling inside us all was the spirit of a female ancestor. Our *fylgja* was a guardian, inseparable and distinct, who guided our steps and watched over us. I liked that. Their belief that human shells could transform into other animals, I liked that too. When I'd last lain in the forest and drifted off, I was a bird with human eyes.

Wandering around the cathedral, I spent some time trying to draw an old stone tablet of a woman, an hourglass and a skull. While sketching the crescent moon carved beside the skull's eye socket, a custodian sidled up to me. He said the carving was dedicated to a woman named Mary Young. He asked if I knew what the moon in the skull was doing there. I shook my head. 'They used to carve those so the souls of the dead could escape,' he whispered.

I thanked the man for his time and went back outside. I walked to the hostel I'd spent the night in. I picked up my backpack and took the bus to Stromness—my memories of childhood summers on the island were sweeping in and out like tides.

I got off at the main pier, and walked between shoppers and tourists until I was at the campsite on the edge of town.

Once I finished setting up my tent, I stood by the sea.

I had to suck on a strand of hair just to calm myself down. The isle of Hoy across the water was catching the light like a luminous green iceberg.

All the terror and beauty of the human world lay there.

Betty Corrigall got pregnant on Hoy in the eighteenth century. That would have been okay if she'd been married. But she got knocked up by a whaler while unwed. He had gone off and left her, so she was in the worst position imaginable. Being unwed and unattached in a Christian community then was akin to a death sentence. It was for her. She was ejected from the community.

Now, it can be wonderful going off to live alone as a woman if it's what you want. If it's a choice it can be beautiful. But if you're cast aside without choice, that's a terrible thing. Betty could not just nip off to the shop to purchase some fish and then get a job in a local hotel. There were no shops. There were no hotels. And Hoy is no lush paradise. It wasn't like she could sunbathe like a lizard and live on fruits and tubers. On what fruits? On what tubers? Betty needed the others to survive, and now they were casting her out. At the age of twenty-seven, Betty tried to hasten the inevitable.

Her dress heavy, her tears mixing with salt water—the men spotted her. They rushed into the sea and dragged her onto the sand.

On her second attempt, this time by rope, she died.

Her body was chucked in a peat bog.

A hundred and fifty years later, she was discovered by peat diggers on the moor.

Her body was dredged up again in the Second World War.

All those lonely soldiers stationed by some freezing bog with no women around for miles. Was it fun for them to find a woman's body so well preserved? Was she a bronze dream to them? They referred to her as the Lady of Hoy. They were digging her body up so regularly that her preserved corpse was rapidly disintegrating.

Some higher-ups put a stop to all that. She was chucked back in the bog again.

An American priest named Reverend Kenwood Bryant got wind of Betty's story. He was saddened by the way she'd been treated. He led an effort to give Betty Corrigall a proper headstone. Since the 1970s she's had a grave beside a lochan.

Turning away from the sea, I went to the campsite's common room with my laptop. I did some kitten work. A few hours later, I went out along the main street. I looked in houses with bare windowsills and curtains closed. I looked at others with clouds of dried seaweed and sea urchins on display. I walked past the old rice warehouse, past the house of the shipwreck survivor, past old Mrs. Humphrey's house.

Terrible pulsing stories were everywhere and the sea was lapping at the stone piers. Starlings were flitting about the lamp posts, and the wool shop, the bookshop, the pharmacy, the deli were all bustling; the paper shop I'd never seen before. It sold various items, mainly bookbinding tools. One of the apprentices found me looking at a piece of paper in an open drawer. She wore short blue boots. She nodded at the paper and pointed out a pencil marking in its bottom right corner. 'That's the year the paper was made in,' she said. 'Take it.'

I became suddenly afraid of something of value being in my possession and care. If someone phoned me up while I was half in a dwam? I'd be listening while pulling the lid off the green fountain pen. In no time I'd be absent-mindedly drawing fleas on the oldest paper I'd ever handled. No, I couldn't take care of paper like this. I'd have to give it back.

I sat with a ginger kitten outside the chip shop. Her tail was swinging. My legs were swinging too. I watched the woman from the paper shop walk quickly down the street in one direction. She came back with a 99. She ate her ice cream beside the cat and me. She said she and her boyfriend were separating. She didn't know if she should stay on the island. I said I always dreamed of being alone by this sea, but in reality I thought I'd grow afraid of myself. She responded that Orkney was beautiful, but it could be isolating. I tried to give her back the piece of paper but she wouldn't have it.

I went into the bookshop and bought a copy of *The Elder Edda*. I walked to the museum. I looked at stuffed little auks, ivory combs, at beaded bags brought back by fur trappers; God knows how they procured them. In a glass cabinet was a whalebone figurine that had been unearthed at Skara Brae. It was carved with wide-set eyes and an O for a mouth. It was five thousand years old.

Opposite the museum was Great-Uncle's flat. A blue plaque on the wall stated '1921 to 1996'. Looking up at those windowpanes, I imagined him still up there—a flickering storm lantern. Darkening. Then glowing.

When he was young, he'd named all the children he'd like to have with his future wife—they had Orcadian names like Ingibjorg and Freya—but I suppose it was not to be.

At one point he thought he was going to live at Pluscarden Abbey, but I suppose he had a change of heart about that.

Perhaps he wasn't always sure about his decisions, or the life fated for him. But I think his life was such a good one, such a rich one.

People were always knocking at George's door; he was quite famous and he never would turn away a stranger. One day, when he was in his sixties, a beautiful young artist knocked. Her name was Kenna Crawford. She was a jeweller who could make sand eels out of silver.

How quickly their bond was forged. Kenna stayed in Orkney for some time. She stayed at George's, for their connection was instantly strong and they enjoyed the same things—such as combing the shore and humouring the local women who watched them from a distance, trying to understand their relationship.

George seriously felt Kenna had been lured to the island. He'd written, 'There's no doubt that your ancestors were waiting—have been this long while—to welcome you.'

When I reached the campsite again, it had begun to drizzle. In the common area, a bronzed and elegant older man in a black polo neck and dress shoes was sitting rolling cigarettes. He said normally he took summers off from the university. But this time he'd decided to take on a job working breakfasts at a hotel by Smoo Cave in Sutherland. 'That's why I only have these brogues with me,' he said sadly, kicking up his heels.

He wasn't sure about going back to Oxford, he didn't want to be in the city anymore. He thought he might stay in Orkney actually. Someone with a holiday house on one of the remoter islands—on Papay, maybe, or Sanday?—might want a winter caretaker. He'd tend the fire. He'd treat the old walls with lime. He'd fix the roofs and re-build the stone walls. I asked how it felt to perform such labours. 'I've no idea,' he said. 'I've never tried.' He licked his cigarette closed and put it with the others. 'I'm like a little boy,' he said. 'I imagine doing all these things. I want adventure. At the same time I just want to go home.'

I said I knew just what he meant.

I finished the rest of my work in my tent. Near dusk, I fell asleep with my laptop open by my feet. A storm came in the night. On waking in the morning, I saw a corner of the computer screen had darkened. I held my finger down on the top right button for twenty seconds to force its shutdown.

At breakfast I found the man from Oxford in the common area. Groundwater had crept into his tent too. I made him a tea and asked if I could send an email from his phone. I typed out a message to my boss to say I couldn't work today then pressed send. It was my first full day off since Christmas. I was elated.

I took the passenger ferry from Stromness to Hoy.

On the boat, I bought a Cup-a-Soup from the vending machine. I sat inside the tiny cabin. I fantasised about throwing my laptop into the sea, watching it skip like rocks then disappear. I did up my raincoat. Three of us got off at Moanness pier. We each gave five pounds to a man named Colin. He was waiting in a school bus near the dock to pick up walkers.

Colin looked at his passengers in the rear-view mirror while we drove through the wet valley. He asked us where we were from.

The others answered

Yorkshire,
London.

When I answered, Colin laughed and said, 'But where really?'

'Aberdeenshire, but my family are from—'

'You don't sound like—'

'For the past eight years I've been living in Canada.'

He grinned.

I drummed my fingers against the window and said, 'I'd probably start sounding like the sea in a week if you left me here.'

He nodded seriously then said, 'That's right.'

'When I first moved to Canada people often couldn't understand what I was saying. I suppose I spoke quickly. That was part of it. But there was also my accent. It was upsetting, seeing people straining when I tried to talk. Hearing them say *sorry could you repeat that? Sorry I didn't catch that?* I suppose that felt terrible. Echoing an accent is a way of getting our meaning across more easily. And so I began to subconsciously echo others. Instead of saying wa-er and bu--er, I started enunciating my Ts. I was pronouncing my Ts as Ds. *Can you pass me the budder? May I have a glass of wadder?* Sometimes I still want to lash out and say "your budder tastes awful and your cows are being fed with the derivatives of palm oil." I know that changing my accent probably doesn't say anything good about me. We don't generally like hearing those who are adept at mimesis. It makes us question their integrity. *Who do they think they are? A bloody starling?* Yet I'm not the only one doing it. Seals are doing it.'

'You're not a seal though,' Colin said.

'I wish I was.'

'No you don't.'

'No I don't,' I said, looking down at my coat zipper. 'My great-grandfather was a great mimic,' I said. 'Maybe my mimesis comes from him.'

Colin asked who my great-grandfather was. He said his grandfather would have known him. Thinking about our relatives knowing each other made the both of us suddenly very excited; we were suddenly speaking very fast.

On reaching Rackwick, the hikers went up to see the Old Man of Hoy and I went down alone to see the abandoned crofts on the shore. The cliffs wrapped the bay like great wings. I stood at their centre and watched the thrashing ocean. I ate my banana. I couldn't hold in my excitement at being in Rackwick any longer. The whole valley before me and it looked just like the Sylvia Wishart painting I had as my computer wallpaper.

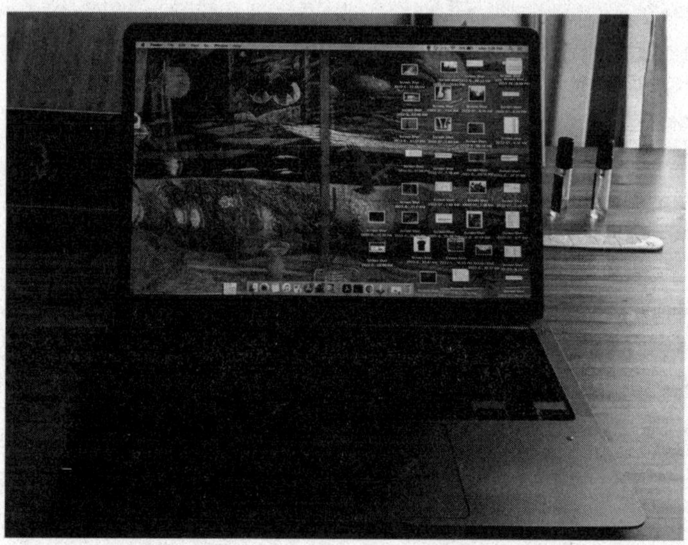

But so much bigger.

It was a ruined croft when Sylvia bought North-house in Rackwick in the 1960s. She restored it then set about capturing this whole bay. Her materials were oils and gouache, pastels, sand grains, white lead, and cigarette ash.

Sylvia painted the sea all scrambled up with her window reflections. She painted textures of bracken falling like wine. She painted riptides and lichen and murky rabbits and dancing curtains till the outside became part of the inside, till each was suffused and essential to the other.

Three pears pierced boats on the ocean. A glimmer of moon lay on a table as a reflection. The very near and very far are always touching.

Of her painting style, Sylvia once explained, 'A friend dropped in when I was out, and with a felt tip pen drew on the window, amongst other things, a bird. This for the first time made me consciously look at the window, as well as through it and led to a series of paintings including this bird. I never washed it off, it just faded away. And ever since, that has led to a fascination with images found on the window pane, beyond and behind, leading inevitably to that ambiguity of space that has always held me.'

Sylvia grew up in the council house next to my granny and her brothers; she always seemed to find a home with excellent views of the sea. I think the sea was compelling her to live near it. I think they had a profound relationship. For the sea gave back, and then some. The sea played endlessly for Sylvia. She was a river of blue creation in its presence.

Sylvia lived alone. She had big parties. She painted the waves on sheets of paper she'd tack to the wall. With a brush in one hand and a fag in the other, she'd let each painting grow in all directions. She decided where they stopped.

Long time now since the valley contained a thriving community. Since the green slopes were dotted with family crofts, with people who lived by the movements of the sun and fish.

Rackwick was a close community for centuries. The Industrial Revolution hardly touched the people's way of living. The people lived in the bay much as their ancestors had even as life on the mainland was drastically changing.

Then at the end of the nineteenth century a Kirkwall merchant bought five sailing smacks and turned them into sailing shops. He began sending them to hard-to-reach places. For sale on *The Gleaner* was tea, sugar, and other exotic sundries. Villagers could buy them with peat-cured fish, eggs, and knitted stockings. It took a while for new shopping habits to be created. 'The notion of progress is not easy to take root in an elemental community; the people are conservative, cling hard to tradition which is their only sure foothold and the ground of all their folk wisdom and art and of the precarious crafts by which they lived,' Great-Uncle wrote of the changes.

Gradually, the people of Rackwick developed an appetite for the items on sale. The 'gifts of progress' came to the village in the form of rubber boots, primus stoves, novels, newspapers, lemonade, Tilley lamps, cloth caps, bicycles, fly papers, cough mixture, marmalade. A gramophone came to the village and 'the fiddle hung on the wall like a dry chrysalis'. The new items aroused in the people a new feeling of avarice.

'The notion of progress is a cancer that makes an elemental community look better,' George wrote, 'and induces a false euphoria, while it drains the life out of it remorselessly.'

And so it was that the young folk began to feel that working in an office or shop might be superior to the community's 'dung and fish-gut trades' that now made them so ashamed.

The youth left the valley. The crofts were slowly abandoned. By the 1960s, the year-round population had diminished to one solitary household—home to Jack Rendall the farmer. Then Sylvia came and fixed up a house. And Peter Maxwell Davies came and fixed up a house. He wasn't from Orkney. He grew up in Manchester and found success as an avant-garde composer.

Initially, he'd come to Orkney on a holiday to see St. Magnus Cathedral. On his second day, he visited Rackwick. Great-Uncle and some pals were there having a rammy. It was a dreich day. Yet to Max, it was immediately clear this place was special.

The sea's hush and boom—it could be almost overwhelming to him.

The shoof and hush of the sea now, these frequencies and overtones. Raking chords of sea shingle, cliffs crying out and beating the rocks. And one dead bird here on the rocks. No feathers or flesh. Its spine bones very small and shaped like shrunken ram's skulls. The memory of his hands moving warm against the back of my neck as I undo the knot holding my pendant in place and add a bone to the string.

The last time I was here, my husband and I had just married. I'd driven us up to Thurso so we could take the short crossing from there to Stromness. Over the course of a week, we ate at the houses of various family members of mine. We climbed inside a Neolithic tomb that had been recently discovered, filled with the ancient bones of humans and otters mixed together. We piled bikes on the boat to Hoy and cycled to Dwarfie Stane.

That megalithic chambered tomb was carved five thousand years ago. Those who hollowed it, scraping stone against stone, were able to make an opening about three feet square. The opening led to an inner chamber. In 1850 an eccentric named Captain William Mounsey had a reckoning there. He carved 'I have sat two nights and so learnt patience' on the walls in Persian calligraphy. Then he wrote his name backwards, in Latin.

Great-Uncle thought Rackwick would not remain with just a few households forever. He wrote, 'It could happen that the atom-and-planet horror at the heart of our civilisation will scatter people again to quiet beautiful fertile places of the world.'

Yet there's just one burn providing fresh water to the whole valley. And when it dries up, what then? Desalination tanks? And after that? Already there are droughts happening in Orkney. The reservoirs providing water to both Kirkwall and Stromness are the lowest they've ever been.

When I got back to the mainland, I washed my face and went for tea at cousin Irina's. She served a fish pie. She said there were quite a few folk living in Rackwick now. She told me about one man there who loved clocks. They were all over his home and in his garden—had I not noticed? Some years ago, he'd been wheeling a huge clock in a wheelbarrow through Stromness when a group of wandering Americans had wondered at his set-up and asked what he was doing. He looked down sadly at his clock and replied, 'I couldn't afford a watch.' Then he started laughing maniacally and carried on.

She said when Peter Maxwell Davies became too old for the steep slopes of Rackwick, he moved to the low isle of Sanday and composed there. When the police came round one day to seize a dead swan on his land (it had flown into a nearby electric line; he'd called to let the RSPB know), he said with quiet geniality that the primary school children needed fresh angel's wings for their nativity play, and anyway swan terrine tasted quite marvellous—like pheasant mixed with venison. Would they like to try some? If the police then reminded him that all swans in the British Isles belonged to the Crown, I imagine Max had fun stating that, as the Master of the Queen's Music, he rather hoped her royal highness might forgive him.

I asked Irina if she would ever move to Rackwick. She said, 'I am happy just where I am.'

After dinner, I walked out of town and up the coast to the graveyard. Yesterday my husband called to talk about three bear cubs he'd just seen climbing up a tree. He'd tried to tell his coworkers about the encounter, but found it was hard to project the feeling of beauty with just a few words.

I looked at headstones carved with the names of generation after generation of vanished men—sea captains and lighthouse keepers, Hudson's Bay boys and deckhands Drowned in Wick and Lost at Sea and Fallen at the Battle of Passchendaele.

One family's headstone listed dead infant after dead infant after dead infant after dead infant after dead infant after dead infant, then two grown-up children.

One listed a wife, and here was a wife and mother, a wife and mother, a dear aunt and daughter, a wife, a wife, a dearest daughter, a dearest daughter, dearest daughter, dearest daughter, dearest daughter, dearest daughter, dearest daughter, and here was Great-Granny, and here was Great-Grandfather. And to their right, the youngest of their sons laid to rest beside them. His headstone was speckled with lichen. I traced a finger across the furred letters,

Carve The Runes Then Be Content With Silence

Would his mother and father be touched to see the array of mementos left by his grave? There was a small stone maze leading to the name Julian of Norwich, a terracotta tile saying 'All Will Be Well', mounds of little pebbles, bits of feather and twig, a toy koala on a string.

When he'd met Kenna the jeweller, George felt a summons from the past had brought her to Orkney. He felt sure she should stay. In their correspondence after she travelled back home to Edinburgh, he'd written to her,

'Now she has found a way
Back to the hills and sea

Of her people, and discovered
Seals on the shore, waiting.'

Those words felt real to me.

Photo credits

Softs

To Pastures New, by James Guthrie (© Aberdeen City Council, Art Gallery & Museums Collections)

Dolly Crombie, by Robert Brough (© Aberdeen City Council, Art Gallery & Museums Collections)

The Gleaner, by Jules Breton (© Aberdeen City Council, Art Gallery & Museums Collections)

Hirta

Margaret Fay Shaw (National Trust for Scotland)

Margaret Fay Shaw (National Trust for Scotland)

Bare feet being compared (National Trust for Scotland)

St Kilda cleit (Bob Jones/Wikimedia Commons/CC BY-SA 2.0)

Margaret Fay Shaw (National Trust for Scotland)

Margaret Fay Shaw (National Trust for Scotland)

Skate

Christiane and Hermann Ritter (Bjørn Klauer/Huskyfarm/ Karin Ritter)

Dandelion

Owlet (Mike's Birds/Wikimedia Commons/CC BY-SA 2.0)

Kindling

Monastic cells (Geo24/Wikimedia Commons/CC BY-SA 3.0)

Hoy

Mary Young tablet (MichaelMaggs; cropped/Wikimedia Commons/CC BY-SA 4.0)

Betty Corrigall's grave (Peter Ward/Wikimedia Commons/CC BY-SA 2.0)

Sylvia Wishart (From the Ernest Walker Marwick Photographic Collection © Orkney Library & Archive)

Dwarfie Stane (Grovel/Wikimedia Commons/CC BY-SA 3.0)

Stone inscription (Bruce McAdam/Wikimedia Commons/CC BY-SA 2.0)

All other images are either the author's or in the public domain.

Source notes

Epigraph

The Annie Ernaux quote from *The Years*, trans. Alison L. Strayer (2017), is included with permission from Seven Stories Press.

Intro

Tanonius Marcellinus's story is described by the classicist Peter Toohey in *Boredom: A Lively History* (Yale University Press, 2012).

The idea of seeing the world anew by looking upside down through the legs comes from Nan Shepherd's *The Living Mountain* (Aberdeen University Press, 1977). What was Shepherd up to, in her day? Striding over moors, sleeping on rocks, feeling in every inch 'how grand it is to get leave to live'.

Slammakin

When the narrator writes of oxygen affecting people's brain chemistry at high altitude, she is referencing Shami Kanekar et al.'s study titled 'Hypobaric Hypoxia Induces Depression-like Behavior in Female Sprague-Dawley Rats, but Not in Males', *High Altitude Medicine & Biology* (March 2015), https://doi.org/10.1089/ham.2014.1070.

Seals' response to music has been documented by various researchers, including Amanda L. Stansbury and Vincent M. Janik at the University of St. Andrews in 'Formant Modification Through Vocal Production Learning in Grey Seals' (those seals, with practice, could 'sing' 'Twinkle Twinkle Little Star'), *Current Biology* (June 2019), https://doi.org/10.1016/j.cub.2019.05.071.

Softs

Jacqueline Riding writes in detail about the life of the Jacobite prince in 'Bonnie Prince Charlie: Scottish Superhero or Italian Coward?', *BBC History*, January 2022.

The entire six-volume series of the *Carmina Gadelica* is available to read as a single edition through Floris Books (1992). Volumes 1 to 3 can also be read online through the Internet Archive.

Berries

The narrator is quoting a passage from the novel *Voyage in the Dark* by Jean Rhys (W.W. Norton, 1994) when describing how 'Their glassy eyes that don't admit anything so definite as hate . . .'

Inga learned about Siberians heading for the woods to go mushroom foraging after the Soviet Union's collapse from anthropologist Anna Lowenhaupt Tsing's book *The Mushroom at the End of the World: On the Possibility of Life in Capitalist Ruins* (Princeton University Press, 2015).

The ancient Greek saying 'live as though all your ancestors were living again through you' reached modern audiences through the letters of Ted Hughes.

The narrator learned about a pioneer miner who had a family composed of various pets in historian Susan J. Matt's book *Homesickness: An American History* (Oxford University Press, 2011).

Hirta

The story of Neil and Mary Ann is based on records about St Kilda cited in Tom Steel's book *The Life and Death of St. Kilda* (Fontana Books, 1975). The section where Mary Ann knifes at rats behind the house wallpaper is inspired by a passage in Margaret Fay Shaw's memoir *From the Alleghenies to the Hebrides: An Autobiography* (Birlinn, 2008).

The letter signed by the islanders, requesting government assistance to leave St Kilda, is listed in public records as '10 May 1930 National Records of Scotland, Agriculture and Fisheries files, AF57/26/3'.

Clara

That birds may age faster in noisy areas is described in Adriana Dorado-Correa et al.'s study 'Timing Matters: Traffic Noise Accelerates Telomere Loss Rate Differently Across Developmental Stages', *Frontiers in Zoology* (August 2018), https://doi.org/10.1186/s12983-018-0275-8.

Acoustic ecologist Gordon Hempton describes how noise can affect humans in the article 'The quietest place in the US', *BBC Travel*, February 2022. 'Noise pollution shortens lives,' he says. 'It's the new second-hand smoke.'

Noise-induced sleep fragmentation is explored in various studies, including Mathias Basner et.al., 'Single and Combined Effects of Air, Road, and Rail Traffic Noise on Sleep and Recuperation', *Sleep* (2011), https://doi.org/10.1093/sleep/34.1.11.

The manifesto Clara reads in bed is *The Art of Noises: Futurist Manifesto* by Luigi Russolo del (1913), trans. Robert Filliou insert (1913) (© Estate of Robert Filliou / Courtesy Estate of Robert Filliou & Peter Freeman, Inc. New York / Paris). A facsimile of the pamphlet is available through the non-profit Primary Information.

John Cage compared burglar alarms to Brâncuşi sculptures while talking with Stephen Montague in 'John Cage at Seventy: An Interview', *American Music*, Summer 1985.

Sei

The John Daido Loori story is from his book *The Zen of Creativity: Cultivating Your Artistic Life* (Ballantine Books, 2005).

The Sei Shōnagon lines are from *The Pillow Book*, trans. Meredith McKinney (Penguin Classics, 2007).

Beaver

The astronomer Galileo Galilei's satirical poem 'Capitolo contro il portar' was written in 1590, while he was the poorest paid mathematics lecturer at the University of Pisa (and salty about the university's plans to impose fines on staff who did not wear their prescribed gowns).

The passage on hoarding is inspired by Lonny Douglas Meinecke's paper 'Hoarding: Emotionally Preparing for a Cognitive Winter' (2012), Grand Canyon University, Arizona.

The 'real & eternal World' quote is from William *Blake's Jerusalem: The Emanation of the Giant Albion* (1804–1820).

Blueberry

The cookbook by René Redzepi is *The Noma Guide to Fermentation* (Artisan, 2018), co-written with chef and photographer David Zilber.

Stew

The Al Jazeera article 'Stars Seize Iranian Imagination' (October 2005) describes street lights in Saadat Shah being turned off for stargazing events. The municipalities of Greater Geneva, the town of Franeker in the Netherlands, and the city of Reykjavík have also all, at some point, switched off the street lights so those who are awake might better see the night sky.

Solstice

Christopher S. Wood writes about how the fifteenth-century German scholar Conrad Celtis thought he'd found 'sculpted portraits of Druid priests and monasteries of the druids teeming in the forest', when, actually, he'd come across the former site of a Christian monastery, in *Forgery, Replica, Fiction: Temporalities of German Renaissance Art* (University of Chicago Press, 2008).

The 'look inside your heart' signs lead to Daihikaku Senkōji Temple in Arashiyama, Kyoto.

Yule

Isabelle Eberhardt's life is further described in *The Passionate Nomad: The Diary of Isabelle Eberhardt* (Virago, 1987) and in Annette Kobak's biography, *Isabelle: The Life of Isabelle Eberhardt* (Virago, 2006).

Alexandra David-Néel wrote many books, but the one that focuses on her trip through Tibet is *My Journey to Lhasa: The Classic Story of the Only Western Woman Who Succeeded in Entering the Forbidden City* (Harper Perennial, 2005).

Skate

The Christiane Ritter quotes are from her memoir *A Woman in the Polar Night*, trans. Jane Degras (Pushkin Press, 2019).

Zhivago

'The more suns there are in the sky, the colder the air is' refers to sun dogs, or parhelia, which develop as light gets refracted through ice crystals—creating the appearance of false suns directly to the left and right of the actual sun. Sometimes, when it's very cold, a halo of light arcing through those sun dogs in a complete circle can create the appearance of there being five suns in the sky.

The journalist George Monbiot describes giving up flying because he could no longer justify it in his article 'On the Flight Path to Global Meltdown', *The Guardian*, 21 September 2006.

Strena seu de nive sexangula by Johannes Kepler was published in English as *The Six-Cornered Snowflake*, trans. Colin Hardie (Oxford University Press, 1966).

Aroma

Paul Rezendes describes how to read animal signs in *Tracking and the Art of Seeing: How to Read Animal Tracks and Signs* (Collins

Reference, 1999). 'Tracking an animal is opening a door to the life of that animal,' he writes. 'It is an educational process, like learning to read. It is learning to read.'

The study observing PMS-like symptoms in baboons is by Glenn Hausfater and Barbara Skoblick, 'Perimenstrual behavior changes among female yellow baboons: Some similarities to premenstrual syndrome (PMS) in women', *American Journal of Primatology* 9 (1985), https://doi.org/10.1002/ajp.1350090302.

Bear

Patricia Van Tighem described being attacked by a bear in Waterton Lakes National Park in her book *The Bear's Embrace: A Story of Survival* (Anchor, 2005).

Charlie Russell and Maureen Enns's experiences in the Russian Far East are further described in their book *Grizzly Heart: Living Without Fear Among the Brown Bears of Kamchatka* (Random House Canada, 2002).

Path

The parable about the bear destroying the garden comes from Margery Kempe's late medieval autobiography *The Book of Margery Kempe*, ed. B.A.Windeatt (The Folio Society, 2004).

Morel

Information on when to pick morels so their spores can be effectively dispersed comes from the 2007 U.S. Forest Service General Technical Report by David Pilz et al., titled 'Ecology and Management of Morels Harvested from the Forests of Western North America'.

Kindling

Michel Louge et al. are the authors of 'Water Vapor Transport Across an Arid Sand Surface—Non-Linear Thermal Coupling, Wind-Driven Pore Advection, Subsurface Waves, and Exchange with the Atmospheric Boundary Layer, a study describing how sand dunes 'breathe'. *Journal of Geophysical Research: Earth Surface* (2022), https://doi.org/10.1029/2021JF006490.

Mosquitoes

Female mosquitoes have a stylet 'tongue' for drinking blood. It contains twenty-five neurons, half of which get very excited during this process of drinking, according to Veronica Jové et al. in 'Sensory discrimination of Blood and Floral nectar by *Aedes aegypti* Mosquitoes', *Neuron* (2020), https://doi.org/10.1016/j.neuron.2020.09.019.

The quote 'I thought, if only I could marry I should have nothing but song and dancing' comes from *A Celtic Miscellany: Translations from the Celtic Literature*, trans. Kenneth Hurlstone Jackson (Penguin Classics, 1972).

Wedding

While a worm has no eyes, it does have Lichtzellen receptor cells across its body that can sense whether it's light or dark. Yale researchers have also studied eyeless worms that seem able to sense the colour blue. D.D. Ghosh et al., 'C. *elegans* Discriminates

Colors to Guide Foraging', *Science* (2021), https://doi.org/10.1126/science.abd3010.

The section about a 'religion of smug ease' affecting the masses comes from Friedrich Nietzsche, *The Gay Science*, trans. Thomas Common (1882).

Common seals have an excellent sense of hearing underwater, but even on land they respond to sounds from 1 to 22.5 kHz (the average human hearing range is from 0.02 to 20 kHz), according to Colleen Reichmuth et al. in 'Comparative Assessment of Amphibious Hearing in Pinnipeds', *Journal of Comparative Physiology* A (2013), https://doi.org/10.1007/s00359-013-0813-y.

The artist referenced in the chapter 'Wedding' is Hanna Tuulikki, whose work includes *Air falbh leis na h-eòin – Away with the Birds*—a body of work exploring the mimesis of birds in Gaelic song—and *Seals'kin*, a sonic and choreographic meditation on loss, longing, transformation, and kinship, shot on location in coastal Aberdeenshire.

Hoy

The quote from Father Benedict comes from the article 'Force of Habit: The Struggles Facing the Monks of Pluscarden Abbey', *The Scotsman*, 2012.

The information about *fylgja* guardians is from Neil Price's *Children of Ash and Elm: A History of the Vikings* (Basic Books, 2020).

Many of the details about the life of George Mackay Brown were gleaned from his *For the Islands I Sing: An Autobiography* (Birlinn,

1997) and Maggie Fergusson's *George Mackay Brown: The Life* (John Murray, 2006).

The Sylvia Wishart quote comes from 'Sylvia Wishart: An Artist in Her Places', an essay by Mel Gooding in the Pier Arts Centre publication *Sylvia Wishart – A Study* (© 2012, Pier Arts Centre, Orkney).

Notes on social changes in Rackwick over the years come from George Mackay Brown, *An Orkney Tapestry* (Victor Gollancz, 1969), illustrated by Sylvia Wishart. Quotes are included by permission of the Literary Estate of George Mackay Brown.

Biographical notes on Peter Maxwell Davies are taken from the article 'How Swan Terrine Landed Queen's Composer on the Wrong Side of the Law', *The Guardian*, 18 March 2005.

Acknowledgements

Parts of this novel were originally published, in different forms, in *Longreads*, *Folio Literary Journal*, *The Guardian*, and *Orion*. The Canada Council for the Arts and the Alberta Foundation for the Arts have supported the writing of the book.

© Schae Photography

AILSA ROSS writes about people, place, and art for *Outside*, *Orion*, *The Guardian*, and others. She grew up in the north of Scotland and lives in the Canadian Badlands. This is her first novel.

Ailsaross.com
X: @ailsa_writes
Instagram: @ailsa_ross